Also by Barbara Ashton

Changing Lifestyles

Miska Valley

Barbara Ashton

BALBOA.
PRESS
A DIVISION OF HAY HOUSE

Balboa Press books may be ordered through booksellers or by contacting:

Balboa Press
A Division of Hay House
1663 Liberty Drive
Bloomington, IN 47403
www.balboapress.com.au
1 (877) 407-4847

Because of the dynamic nature of the Internet, any web addresses or links contained in this book may have changed since publication and may no longer be valid. The views expressed in this work are solely those of the author and do not necessarily reflect the views of the publisher, and the publisher hereby disclaims any responsibility for them.

The author of this book does not dispense medical advice or prescribe the use of any technique as a form of treatment for physical, emotional, or medical problems without the advice of a physician, either directly or indirectly. The intent of the author is only to offer information of a general nature to help you in your quest for emotional and spiritual well-being. In the event you use any of the information in this book for yourself, which is your constitutional right, the author and the publisher assume no responsibility for your actions.

Any people depicted in stock imagery provided by Thinkstock are models, and such images are being used for illustrative purposes only. Certain stock imagery © Thinkstock.

Print information available on the last page.

ISBN: 978-1-4525-2994-3 (sc)
ISBN: 978-1-4525-2995-0 (e)

Balboa Press rev. date: 07/15/2015

Chapter One

Margaret and Richard Paterson had built up a very successful furniture-manufacturing business in Banora Point, near the border of New South Wales and Queensland. Richard had employed a few loyal and very good carpenters over the years, and Margaret had studied interior design to help with the latest trends in home decorating.

They raised two children. Their son, Andrew, was tall and blond-haired with blue-grey eyes; he was a successful accountant and had recently accepted a very good offer to join the accounting firm of Harlow, Smith & Co. in Coolangatta. Owing to the sophistication of technology, he did a lot of his computer work at home. Their daughter, Gail, was of medium build with blue eyes and light brown hair, and she had a very friendly nature. Gail had always been a very caring person and decided to study the humanities, which resulted in her working for Docs. Many sad cases of child neglect followed.

When Gail met Brett, a muscular guy with sandy hair and brown eyes, she thought he was the man for her. They married and decided to buy a run-down, twelve-room motel on the highway from the Gold Coast to Brisbane. It was built on a small parcel of land with a narrow strip of grass near the front, and it had enough turning space for visitors' cars in front of the units. Brett, with the help of Andrew and Richard, had turned the first unit into a double-storey manager's home and office. They renovated the remaining eleven units into very attractive living areas for the customers.

Gail set to making the small strip of land at the front a very attractive garden; she also planted small palm trees near the entrance to each unit. "I will enjoy working in the office now; it was a bit dreary before," she told Brett. "We will have to employ some part-time staff to clean the units each morning." "Yes and I will be able to do the entire garden and yard maintenance."

Brett felt sure that they could manage between them.

After twelve years they had a very successful business. During this time, Gail had become very involved with disadvantaged children. The couple sometimes used vacant units for emergencies when the police or child-welfare agents rang—usually in the dead of night—to tell her that another child had to be removed from the parents' home because of sexual or physical abuse. Gail found it necessary to sleep in the unit after pacifying the child and waiting for the administration to find a suitable foster home. Gail and Brett's son, David, was a strapping lad of ten years, and he attended a private school in Brisbane.

Andrew met Sandra when he starting working at Harlow and Smith's accounting firm. Sandy was a tall, slim woman with short blonde hair, blue eyes, and a very bad temper that she managed to keep hidden most of the time. She had been hoping that a good-looking man—preferably single—would take the vacant position when it was advertised. She had arranged interviews for the applicants, and when Andrew presented himself, she hoped he would be successful. She introduced herself and made sure he was comfortable while he waited. When Mr. Smith came out of his office with Andrew, her expectations rose.

"How did the interview go, Andrew?" Sandy asked.

"Very good, thank you." Andrew couldn't help noticing her grin.

Andrew was besotted with her beautiful eyes and lovely figure. She realised that she had him under her spell and decided that he would be an easy catch if she played her actions carefully. She worked at the reception desk and made a point of greeting Andrew with a beautiful, sexy smile each day when he entered the office. The job was his, and Sandy felt he was hers for the taking.

"Hello, Andrew. Did you have a good weekend? I will make you a delicious hot coffee and bring it to your office in about thirty minutes, okay?"

Andrew was a little surprised, but he accepted her offer and proceeded to his office. He had a busy day ahead of him.

Sandy put the coffee and a few biscuits on a tray, undid the top two buttons on her blouse, and slowly leaned over Andrew's shoulder to put the tray in front of him. "I'll collect the tray shortly," she purred.

"Thank you, Sandy." Andrew noticed the blouse and the very pretty bulge of her breasts, which were barely hidden by her bra.

When Sandy returned for the tray, she leaned over his desk and almost fell out of the blouse. A co-worker entered the office at that moment and pretended not to notice. Sandy hurriedly straightened her back and left his office.

So far, so good, she thought. *Bugger, Peter! Why did he have to spoil it?*

Andrew forced himself to concentrate on the work in front of him. *Sandy is certainly a beautiful woman, and maybe she would like to join me for dinner on Thursday night.* He decided to wait to invite her until tomorrow, after he had given it some more thought.

Andrew didn't need to go to the office on Tuesday. However, he decided to ring Sandy to ask her to dinner on Thursday evening. "Sandy, I am working at home today. I have been thinking about you and wondered if you would like to have dinner with me at a sea-view restaurant on Thursday."

"That sounds like a very pleasant evening. Thank you, sexy."

Sandy started planning her next moves. She knew he had his own apartment in Surfers Paradise. *Now, what should I wear? The little black number or a soft, romantic blue dress with black, saucy underwear?*

She did not see him until Thursday morning, when he arrived at the office. She made him the usual coffee, gave him a wink, and told him where to pick her up at 8:00 p.m. She decided on the blue dress; it had a very low-cut neckline, which allowed her black lace bra to be seen. The slim skirt showed off her long legs in high-heel black shoes, and she carried a black clutch bag with a shoulder strap for security when she danced. The night was warm, the music was soft, and the meal was delicious. Andrew held her close while he hummed to the music. She started to feel very romantic and cuddled up to him, stroking the back of his neck and giving him little kisses.

They decided to leave around eleven, and Andrew asked her if she wanted to go back to his unit for a drink.

"I thought you would never ask," she murmured.

Andrew poured the drinks and switched on romantic music, and they cuddled up on the large sofa. Sandy reached for his shirt and slowly undid the buttons. Andrew unzipped her dress, which fell to the floor, and then he unclipped her lacy bra.

"Oh, Sandy, your breasts feel so soft and warm." He fondled them, which made them both feel very horny. Sandy unzipped his trousers and then stood up to show him her lacy underwear. He sat there for a few moments lapping up the beautiful sight, and then he stood up to grab her in a lustful embrace. He kissed her all over, and then they let their passion take over.

When they woke, the sun was starting to creep through the curtains. Sandy slowly left the sofa and went into the bathroom for a shower and shampoo. Andrew said he would drive her home so she could get ready for work.

"Thank you for a beautiful night," he said.

"Can we do it all again?" she asked.

"Yes, sometime in the future. I have a pretty heavy schedule, you know."

Sandy had other ideas and felt she knew how to arrange it.

Andrew worked from home until the following Monday. Sandy had been plotting all weekend. When she next spoke to Andrew, it was almost all done by eye contact. She made the coffee as usual and made sure her fingers touched his hand. She gave him sexy grins every time she saw him. Her low necklines were a regular turn-on for Andrew, who thought about their first night often. He decided that Sandy was not the type of girl he had in mind to marry, but she was a good plaything in the meantime.

He decided to ask her out at the end of the month. There were quite a few nights after that when Sandy asked him about his family and suggested to him that she would like to meet them. They had been to the beach a few times, and the sight of Sandy in a bikini was mind-boggling; sex always followed at his unit.

Sandy eventually met Andrew's mum and dad. They invited her for Sunday dinner, and she was on her best behaviour and chose a pretty floral sundress to wear. Margaret made a fuss over her and told Andrew that she was a very sweet, pretty girl.

It was about three months after their first date when Sandy told Andrew she was pregnant with his child.

"It can't be mine. I was using condoms, and then you told me that you were on the pill and not to worry."

"Well, I haven't slept with anyone else since I met you, so you must have slipped up somewhere." *The little splits in the condoms must have worked,* she thought.

"I want some proof about paternity; it is not satisfactory for you to just make a statement like that," Andrew said, annoyed.

"All right. We will have to go to see the doctor or family clinic as soon as possible," she stated. She had no doubt in her mind, because she had made sure she had not jeopardised her chances. Andrew had not planned to start a family at this early stage in his career, but he didn't like the prospect of an abortion either. Sandy made the necessary arrangements for DNA testing, and she told Andrew and said that they had to go together next week. After the tests were concluded, they were told that the results would be available shortly. The tests came back positive; Sandy became teary and wrapped her arms around him.

"I don't know what to do, Andrew," she sobbed.

"I will stand by you, Sandy. We will have to face this together."
Andrew felt that he needed to talk to his father about the situation. "Dad, I have been careless and made a huge mistake regarding Sandy. She has become pregnant, and I thought I had taken all precautions."

"Well, son, are you sure that the baby is yours?"

"We have done the necessary DNA tests. Yes, the baby is mine."

Richard explained that Andrew was under no obligation to marry Sandy, but he must do the right thing by her and the baby's future, financially and emotionally. Andrew had a long talk with Sandy and her mother before asking his own mother to join in the discussions. Margaret felt that they cared enough for each other to make the adjustments for a successful marriage. The thought of a beautiful little baby in the family once again was a delight.

When Andrew told his family that a baby was on the way, Gail arranged a dinner so that she could meet Sandy before the wedding took place. She liked her very friendly nature but couldn't help feeling that all was not right.

Sandy's mother was contacted again, and a small family wedding was arranged; Sandy's father had passed away some years earlier.

They settled down to family life, and Christie was welcomed by all. Andrew had grown to love Sandy; she had a lot of good points, and life ran smoothly enough. They decided to increase the family and were delighted when the twins, Jason and Scott, arrived two years later. Gail helped her as much as she could, and Margaret was very willing to babysit on occasions.

Chapter Two

Richard and Margaret felt that retirement was calling when they started looking for an ideal spot not too far from the family so that they could bring the children to visit on school holidays. When they drove into the small valley with the shimmering lake in the middle, they knew that it was made for them. Richard drove to the council the next day to ask about building permits, and then he went to the estate agents to leave a deposit on the small acreage.

"The children are all settled at school and Gail and Andrew are settled into married life." Margaret felt content, It had been six years since the twins arrived

"We want to have the house built on one level with three bedrooms, a large family room, and a lounge and dining room. What do you think, Margaret?"

"Yes, Richard. I would also like an en suite to the main bedroom and a separate bathroom for guests."

"I will contact Peter to draw up some plans for our perusal as soon as possible," Richard said. He was getting excited.

When Peter delivered the plans, he had drawn a separate two-bedroom guest house as well. "I know what it is like with these retirement estates, when the family decides to stay a little longer."

Peter had a lot of experience, and he wanted the best for his good friends.

Richard decided to show Andrew the plans for the house as soon as it could be arranged. They also saw the land and valley. Sandy and the children arrived with him; the twins were a very energetic bundle of enthusiasm like most six year olds.

"Gee, look at this!" cried Scott. "Are you going to buy a boat, Pa?"

"Are there any fish in the lake, Pa?" asked Jason.

All of these questions and more would be answered as time went on; the important thing was to start the process. Sandy and Christie agreed that it was a very pretty area, and they looked forward to spending time there when it was built.

Gail and Brett arranged to view the property in the next week or two, during the school holidays so they could bring David along with them. Gail was very happy with her parents' choice.

"So long as you and Dad are happy, I am happy too," she told them.

David was Gail and Brett's only child, and he attended a private school in Brisbane. He was a year older than the twins, but the four cousins did not spend much time together. Sandy was jealous of the fact that David was at a private school; she often hinted that Richard should pay for their children to attend a private school too. Richard and Margaret spoke about it but decided that the children were progressing well in the public system.

When Gail and Brett arrived at Miska Valley, they fell in love with it. "Oh! It is beautiful, Mum, and Dad will be able to buy a little runabout with an outboard motor so that he can go fishing on the lake."

"What fish can you catch in the lake, Richard?" asked Brett.

"I believe that freshwater perch, however I will talk to our few neighbours to find out more."

"We will have a fibreglass swimming pool put into the ground so that it can be accessed from the family room," Richard told them.

When the plans were approved by the council, they contacted the builder contracted for the go-ahead, and the excitement increased. A BBQ picnic was arranged as the work progressed. Gail brought most of the food, and the two mothers set to preparing a small feast. Sandy wanted to know whether the twins and David could take the boat onto the lake without Richard, but Andrew didn't think that was a very good idea.

The building progressed slowly. Richard put their furniture business on the market for a good price, and he said that they would not sell until they found the right buyer. The estate agent kept them informed of all the offers that came in, and eventually they sold it to a young couple who had a lot of experience in carpentry.

"Well, Andrew, now that they have sold the business, we can ask them for some money to update our cars and get a few things for the house," Sandy said. She was busy thinking about what she could replace.

"Sandy, I can provide everything we need. Don't be so silly. Mum and Dad have worked very hard and deserve a happy retirement."

"Andrew, my car is five years old, and I am thinking of returning to part-time employment soon. A modern car would be better, particularly when I need to drive around the children. Gail has a new car, so I don't see why I have to settle for a bomb," she mumbled.

"Gail has a more modern car because she works for the government, and she has to be available all the time to help with unfortunate children. She has a generous car allowance," Andrew pointed out.

"I'm sick of hearing how much she does for disadvantaged children. What about *our* children?" Sandy's temper was rising, and Andrew knew when to shut up.

Andrew felt that Sandy's life was becoming mundane; maybe she needed to find casual employment. *I will ask Mum if she can mind the children one night next week so that the two of us can have a lovely dinner and maybe go to see a movie. I will have a look at a few new cars also.* Sandy had always been a restless person, but he couldn't understand her obvious envy of Gail. He knew that she loved the children and wanted the best for them. The boys had started playing soccer when they turned five. She took them along to practise twice each week after school, and both Andrew and Sandy watched them play each Saturday morning. Christie had tried a variety of sports: basketball, swimming, and tennis. Tennis was her favourite, which meant more afterschool running from here to there. They all loved the surf; the whole family joined the little nippers, and the children went along each Sunday morning to gain experience on their surfboards. Andrew suggested that Sandy join the Parents and Citizen Association at the children's school, which she did. They were a very active group and worked hard to raise money at fetes and tuck shops, and she met some very good friends who often got together in the evenings. Andrew was happy to look after the children while he caught up on some work on the computer.

Sandy soon started to complain about the fact that they still lived in a unit. "Why can't we move to a big house with a garden and swimming pool?" she moaned.

"I guess it is time to think about a garden. Do you think that gardening would give you some pleasure, Sandy?"

"Yes, it would. Can we go looking on the weekend?"

"Okay," Andrew replied. He felt that Sandy could spend a lot of time getting to know the neighbours when they found a suitable house.

Sandy started to think about her mother. Her mother was getting on in years, and it would be a good idea to have her live with them. *A live-in child carer* she thought. *I will have to work on Andrew so that he thinks it is his idea. It will give me a lot more freedom when I start work again, and she enjoys gardening.* Sandy had had enough of a stay-at-home mothers' life; she wanted some excitement. She still loved Andrew and the children, and she realised that they would eventually have access to Richard and Margaret's money, but that was probably a long way off. However, she had to be careful. Andrew was so wrapped up in his work that they never seemed to go out to glamorous places.

Pam, Sandy's mum, and Andrew agreed that it would be wise for her to live with them when all the negotiations were completed. She settled in to the family situation and spent a lot of time with the children, helping with homework and she was looking forward to the garden when they moved to the new house. Pam also spent a lot of time cooking little snacks for after-school treats. She had brought her beloved Labrador, Goldie, who was six years old and loved going for walks with the children.

Christie eventually wanted to know if she could have a kitten. "I will look after it real well. She can sleep with me, and I am sure that she will enjoy Goldie's company," she insisted.

They chose a tortoiseshell kitten. She was so cute and playful, and everybody loved her. Christie named her Pebbles. Andrew was sure that he had agreed to a happier family life for everyone. Sandy seemed to be far more contented, and Pam went along to the meetings at the school; they both helped with making children's clothes and making cakes for the stalls. Andrew and Sandy managed to have a few nights to themselves, enjoying gourmet dinners and stopover nights at lovely hotels on the Gold Coast.

The whole family piled into the four-wheel-drive vehicle to go to Miska Valley for a barbeque and to help set out gardens where they hoped to plant shrubs and flowers. Gail, Brett, and David arrived with Margaret and Richard. The four ladies found a spot in the shade to set up the rugs and tablecloths for a salad feast. The grass was a bright green and very soft, which provided a good spot for the children to sun bake after they had had a swim in the cool water. David always enjoyed his cousins' company; unfortunately he had to spend a lot of time by himself. Goldie had the time of her life: she chased the children, spent some time splashing in the water, and rested before chasing tennis balls that Jason threw for her.

The boys decided to walk through the surrounding bushes and look for a place to build a tree house. The men decided to follow them when they had been gone for some time, and they were met by Scott running along a track calling out that David had fallen from a tree. Andrew and Brett followed Scott to where David sat holding his right ankle.

"What have you done, David?" Asked Brett.

"I slipped when I tried to go a little higher. I can't seem to stand."

Andrew and Brett helped to lift him up, but he slumped to the ground and complained that it hurt. Brett put him on his shoulders and carried him back to where the girls were clearing away the barbeque.

"What happened?" cried Gail.

"I fell out of the tree, and my ankle hurts a lot," David replied.

Brett put him down onto one of the rugs while Gail grabbed the first aid kit from the car. She felt around his foot, pressed it gently, and felt that nothing was broken. "You will have a very sore ankle for a few days. I will take you to the hospital on the way home to get X-rays." Gail had to keep her first aid skills up to date in case she had to attend to any of the children in her care.

The scenario was what Gail had expected: the doctor said that he would put a strong bandage around the ankle to provide protection, and she would then take him to her local doctor in a few days. He had to rest it as much as possible to let the swelling go down. Margaret was a little distressed and offered to look after him until his ankle was better; David was looking forward to being spoilt for a few days.

Chapter Three

---❦---

G ail was woken by the shrill ring of the telephone at 7:00 a.m. one Wednesday morning in June. Her supervisor from Docs asked her to go to the local hospital. An elderly woman, Doreen, had notified them that a newborn baby had been abandoned on her front porch; it was a beautiful little girl, and she had a large pink jumper wrapped around her and a white bunny rug to keep her warm in the cardboard box. The lady said that she had heard a noise that sounded like a car door being shut very quietly around six o'clock, but she took no notice. It wasn't until the baby started to cry that she had connected the two noises. She had gathered the box to her chest, put it in the lounge, and rang the police.

The two police officers arrived very quickly and asked Doreen to tell them everything that she could, and also to accompany them to the hospital. Doreen did as she was asked. After the baby was handed to a young nurse, she sat down to talk to the female officer and Gail.

"Do you have any idea who the mother could be?" Asked the officer

"Do you know of any girls who live near you who may have been pregnant?" queried Gail.

Poor Doreen tried to think of any young girls who had spoken to her when she was working in her garden; she could see their faces but couldn't recall if any showed signs of being pregnant. "No, I am sorry. I do talk to a few people, mainly about plants, but I can't recall any with problems."

"Never mind Doreen, You have been a big help. The baby is in good health, and we will try to find her mother," Gail assured her. "We will give her a temporary name in the hope that the mother will change her mind and come to collect her. Would you like to suggest a name?"

"How about Cheree?" Suggested Doreen

All three thought that was a good name. Gail arranged for a taxi to take Doreen home. Cheree was taken to the nursery, and plans were made for a press release to the paper for the next morning. A photo of the girl would also be shown on the news that night.

Gail took the baby home with her after three days to give her a loving start in life. Brett shared in all the aspects of caring for a newborn. David thought she was gorgeous and wanted to keep her. Gail explained that if the natural mother didn't come forward in three months, she would be put up for adoption.

Sandy and Christie came to visit, and they both made a fuss of Cheree. Christie brought some toys to amuse her. Margaret was more than happy to give her cuddles and kisses when she stopped by.

"Do you find it hard to hand over the babies when the time is up, Aunty Gail?" Christie asked.

"I feel a little sad at the time, but there are s so many children who need our help."

Cheree's photo was shown about once a week with a plea for the mother to come forward. It was to no avail, and eventually Cheree was given to a lovely couple who had a three-year-old son of their own. They were so pleased and said she completed their family. Gail was glad to have a few good nights' sleep after she had kissed Cheree good-bye. Christie asked her mother if they could look after a baby like Gail did, and Sandy said that she had enough to handle with the twins.

Andrew had kept his promise and signed up for a mortgage to buy the house that they all liked. It had four-bedrooms and was positioned on a very large block at Manly: it had a swimming pool and a lovely landscaped garden. It was close to all amenities, and the children could remain at the same school. A small annex was attached to the side of the house that consisted of one bedroom, a bathroom, a kitchenette, and small sitting room; this would be ideal for Pam. The house was close to Coolangatta for Andrew's work and the children's school. Andrew arranged for his father and Brett to check out everything, and then he decided to bring the three children to look it over before he made a final decision.

"We must ask Gail to give the house the once-over. I hope she will be jealous," Sandy said.

"Please don't show your nasty streak in front of Gail," Andrew begged.

Andrew did his best to keep Sandy's temper hidden for his mother's sake. She loved all the children so much and spoilt them, particularly at Christmas time.

Sandy's mum, Pam, was a very stylish, middle-aged woman; her hair was coloured every month by her favourite hairdresser. She had chosen a light blonde shade, and it was cut and styled regularly. Her eyes were dark brown, and she had the same tall, slim build as her daughter. Her life had been quite sad over the years. Her first husband, Sandy's dad, had been killed in the war, which left Pam to rear Sandy and her two brothers, Barry and Daryl, by herself. She had a very modest house and collected a pension from the Army; however she was not satisfied and decided to look for a new husband to help.

Don came into her life when she started going to dances at a local RSL club. It didn't take Pam long to make him feel that married life would be a good deal. He quite happily accepted the three children, who were in their early teens by this time. The boys both played rugby for local teams; they enjoyed the game, and Don used to play in his young days, which created a bond. Sandy, on the other hand, became quite rebellious to her mother's preoccupation with her new husband. Arguments started to develop over stupid things, which put Don's health at risk.

Barry started to stay out to all hours at the club and he drank far too much. Daryl decided that he would rather try to build a life of his own; he moved to Darwin and found work on a cattle station. They still lived in the modest home that Pam had when George was killed, and she suggested to Don that he should do something about providing a more modern home for the three of them. Don was looking into signing up for a mortgage to please Pam when he had a heart attack. He only lived for a few days after that, and Pam's idea for a new home disappeared for the time being.

Barry had managed to sign up for rugby coaching training with a New South Wales, which meant that he would be leaving Queensland. Sandy quieted down a lot and managed to keep her temper under control most of the time.

Pam was still chasing an elusive dream of stability when she met Shirley and Colin, a married couple with two school age children. She became very friendly with Shirley and helped her with the children, who required help with their homework now and then. She also helped run the two children to sporting events when Colin was too busy. When Shirley started to have fainting spells, she called an ambulance and then told Colin to go to the hospital. The doctors were very concerned about her condition and arranged for a lot of tests to find out what her problem was. Pam did as much as she could to help the couple. Sandy often looked after the children, and Pam cleaned the house when Shirley couldn't cope.

Shirley was called to the doctor's rooms for the results; Colin accompanied her to hear the sad news that she had cancer. They both cried, and Shirley was so worried about the children's future. "Oh, Colin, what will we do? The children are so young?"

"Shirley, the doctor will tell us about treatment for you. I will manage to cook, and maybe we can ask Pam if she can lend a hand."

When Colin asked Pam if she could spare some time to lend a hand, she jumped at the chance. "I will arrange to have a lady come to the house twice a week to clean it for you." The two girls, Heather and Julie, felt that they could manage the washing and ironing between them with Shirley's help when she felt well enough. Colin managed to cook good meals for them all, and with the help of modern appliances the kitchen was soon neat and tidy again. Pam made sure that the children got off to school on time each day. Heather and Julie took charge when their mother was not feeling well enough after her chemo treatment. Their house was a lovely, modern, four-bedroom, brick-and-tile home with all the latest gadgets to make life easier. It was on a large block of land with a well-tended garden. Colin hoped that he could still look after it; otherwise he would have to find a handyman or gardener.

Pam found that Colin was relying on her help more and more as time went on. He asked her to take Shirley for treatment on a regular basis. He had a demanding job, but his employer was sympathetic to his problems. Shirley was not responding to her treatment as well as she might be, and so the doctor told Colin not to expect any miracles. He arranged for the children to spend the school holidays with Shirley's parents in Sydney. She was terribly upset when her parents arrived to take the two girls.

"Please try to rest, darling," her mother begged her. "We will have them home at the end of the two weeks."

Pam spent as much time as she could with Shirley. Colin was very attentive, but the strain was starting to eat away at him: his hair was dry, and his shoulders were starting to droop. His girls did as much as they could, but there was no way that they could comfort him in his time of great need. Pam sensed that his inner self was really struggling.

Colin knocked on Pam's door at lunch time one day. "Oh, Pam, I know that I shouldn't ask you, but I need a big hug."

"Do come in, Colin. It is such a struggle for you."

She put her arms around him, drew him to her chest, and snuggled up to give him her best hug. She didn't stop there, however—she kissed him full on the lips and then pulled him onto the couch. She undid the buttons on his shirt, caressed his chest, and then undid the belt on his trousers.

He pulled back from her, startled by his overwhelmed feelings. "Pam, I need you so much. Please say it is okay."

"Yes, Colin, it is okay. We will go into the bedroom, where we can relax."

They removed their clothes and made love until they both felt satisfied. When they were dressed, Pam made him a lovely coffee and told him that he had to keep their actions a secret. If he ever felt the need again, it was all right with her. Pam had suffered the loss of two husbands and could understand his need. She did not see it as being unfaithful to his wife; she knew that he loved Shirley and the children.

Shirley did not improve after her operation, and they continued with the medication until she felt that her time was up. She chose to spend as much time with the family as possible. Her parents arrived to spend quality time with her, and arrangements were made to make her last few days as happy as possible.

When she took her last breath, all the family was present, and Pam and Sandy took care of everything to do with the wake. Colin had already decided to maintain the house and look after the children in the best way possible. Pam stayed away at a respectable distance to let the three of them manage as best they could, but Heather and Julie arrived at her door quite often to talk about school and other little problems.

Sandy had been observing her mother's behaviour over the years and decided to move into a shared accommodation arrangement with a lady and managed to find a good position with an accounting firm as a receptionist. She couldn't believe her luck when Andrew walked into the office to apply for the vacant position at Harlow, Smith & Co.

Chapter Four

*A*fter the funeral, the family sat down to discuss the best way to look at life through the children's eyes. Shirley's parents admired Colin for wanting to keep the family together, and Colin's parents offered to help whenever possible. They decided to call in Pam and Sandy.

Both sets of parents thanked Pam and Sandy for all the help that they had given Colin and the children during the recent tough times. They gave Pam their contact numbers and said that they would arrange school holiday times. Neighbours stopped by to see the family from time to time and helped whenever possible. The school routines and sporting times carried on as usual, and the girls had a lot of school friends.

Pam made sure that she and Colin spent alone time together whenever possible. She gradually took over running of the family. The children felt that she had been such a good friend to their mother that she could be trusted to take care of all of them, just the way Shirley had done. Pam found it easy to convince Colin that the house was too big for her to do all the housework; the cleaner would still come twice each week. She was a very good cook, and it pleased her to see Colin enjoy his meals. The children obviously enjoyed the meals that she cooked for them and their friends. Life was pretty good, but Pam decided that a more intimate relationship could be forged with a little manipulation on her part.

The first anniversary of Shirley's death had passed when Pam bought herself a beautiful negligee set and suggested to Colin that they have a quiet dinner at home with the children. Then they could leave Heather in charge while Pam and Colin went to a hotel for the night.

Colin asked Heather and Julie if they were happy with the arrangement. What do you think of me taking Pam to see a show at the Excelsior Hotel? We will book a room for the night."

"Yes, dad, We feel that you deserve some relaxing time, and we are very fond of Pam."

When Colin told Pam, she was delighted. *First step passed,* she thought. *Now I can work on the marriage proposal. This house will soon be mine. This is the type of home that I have always wanted. The children will soon go their own ways into the big, wide world, and Colin and I will settle down together.*

Pam arranged an overseas trip to Hawaii for the two of them when the girls went to Shirley's parents' house for the next school holiday. Colin was a little apprehensive about leaving the house, but she told him not to be silly. The flight to Honolulu was long and uncomfortable in economy class, so Pam made up her mind to travel business class next time. *And there will be many "next times,"* she thought. In her mind, she and Colin would see the world.

Pam had watched the dark night turn into a brilliant sunrise as the plane commenced landing at Hawaii. She could see the beaches and excitedly nudged Colin to wake him. "Look, Colin. We have arrived. Isn't it beautiful?"

"Yes, Pam. I had a good sleep. Did you?"

"No. I will have to make up for it later, if we have time." She felt too excited to sleep.

They had booked seven days in the Marriott Resort and Spa. It seemed to take forever to disembark and collect their luggage. Colin collected a baggage cart and wheeled it to the taxi line-up. They were greeted with more frangipani leis and complimentary drinks at the hotel. When they signed in and were given the key to their room, Pam had to put her weary body on the king-sized bed.

"This is heaven, Colin. We can share a shower, put on beach clothes, and then go exploring."

"Okay, Pam. Sounds like a good idea to me."

They spent a lot of days wandering around the shops and beaches and spending most nights wrapped in each other's arms. Pam thought that she would be happy to spend the rest of her live in Hawaii. Colin had caught the travel bug and decided to spend a lot more time travelling around the world.

Colin had spent a lot of money on fabulous holidays; sometimes they took the girls with them, but mostly it was just the two of them. Pam had talked Colin into downsizing after they married, and they drew up new wills discounting all of the children on both sides. When he died as a result of a severe stroke, Pam collected all of his money. The girls had good jobs and were self-sufficient: Heather worked for a large warehouse company in Sydney, and Julie was working for a large group of doctors in Newcastle.

Andrew felt sorry for Pam after losing three husbands in such sorry circumstances, and he thought that some tender loving care from him and Sandy would brighten her life a little. The three children thought that it was a cracker idea, especially with the dog and cat to play with. Sandy of course made sure that Andrew never knew of her mother's manipulating ways.

Life settled down again with the children's activities a lot easier to cope with. Pam and Sandy gradually became good friends with the neighbours, and Pam shared morning teas with a neighbour by the name of Betty. Betty was a widow too, and she liked to keep herself smart, with her wavy grey-blonde hair and her figure trim and taunt just like Pam's. They spent some time at a local gymnasium; Sandy went with them sometimes, but she was looking for casual work.

The lovely home at Miska Valley was starting to look very impressive. Margaret and Richard had moved their special belongings into the guest house and decided to sell all their heavy furniture from Banora Point. They spent many hours in furniture stores to decide just what they wanted. Some of the modern furniture was very nice to look at, but Richard was a bit concerned about stability; he didn't want to have to replace it in a few years. They were renting one of the units from Brett, so there was no hurry to decide. Besides, they were enjoying themselves.

"How about we go to look at boats today, Margaret?"

"Do you know exactly what you want, Richard?"

"No, but I have a good idea. I will ask Andrew and Brett to help me to decide."

Richard had decided not to buy before they were living on the property for security reasons, but they went along to the nearest boat yard to get some ideas. It was amazing to listen to the salesmen with all their offers regarding both the boats and the outboard motors.

"Well, I am more confused than ever," Richard admitted.

"I have no idea about boats and motors, but it was fun looking at them all on display," Margaret said. *I guess it will be fishing rods next,* she thought.

Richard had been given a lot of brochures to look at when they drove back to the unit. He spread them out on the table for Brett and Gail to peruse.

"You will be looking at other sale yards, won't you?" Gail wanted to know.

"Yes. We are enjoying ourselves. We may go up to Hervey Bay for a few days to watch the whales playing."

Margaret was all for a few days at Hervey Bay. They loaded the car and set out the next day. They shared the driving, stopping at a lovely cafe on the way for lunch. They found it easy to book into a motel room at Kulsia. The rooms were built surrounding the lake in the middle, with plenty of trees. They saw a possum and two koalas. The swimming pool was cool and inviting, with lovely lounge chairs all around. They decided to have a siesta after the swim, and then they enjoyed a lovely meal in the spacious dining room. The next day they drove to River Heads to board the whaling boat to go to Fraser Island. The whales dove in and out of the water and came so close that it was almost frightening.

Fraser Island was an adventure with dingos wandering around. They took the four-wheel-drive Pajero on the vehicular ferry for the trip. The salad lunch was most enjoyable, and the next day was spent exploring the town and then the night life on the waterfront. They shared the driving on the return trip and decided that they would do it again soon.

When Sandy heard of the trip to Hervey Bay, she started to pester Andrew to take them there for a holiday, insisting that the children deserved a break; her mother could look after the house and the animals. Needless to say, they all enjoyed themselves, and Andrew took his computer to do some work for the office. Christie found some local boys to flirt with, just like her mother, but it all seemed harmless. The boys enjoyed a lot of ball games. Sandy made up her mind to put in a real effort to find casual work when they arrived home. *I bet Gail can't get time off to go on holidays with her job. All she does is work, and she is on call for Docs all the time. Stupid girl,* she thought.

They had settled into their new home very well. Andrew had arranged for a pool-cleaning company to clean the pool one day each week, and Pam enjoyed the garden. Sandy had a cleaning lady do all the heavy work inside the house, and Andrew mowed the lawn when needed. Pam and Betty spent a lot of time together and were talking about an overseas trip next year. Christie and Pebbles spent most of their time together; Pebbles slept on the end of her bed and was a bundle of energy. The boys took turns bathing Goldie and taking her for walks. Andrew felt that life was pretty good, but Sandy was still very restless.

Margaret and Richard continued their boat and furniture shopping. They eventually decided on mostly white, lightweight furniture to make housekeeping a lot easier. They opted to buy a widescreen television when the family room was built.

Chapter Five

G ail was asked to investigate a potential concern about a family with a teenage daughter. The poor girl had become very quiet over the past month and was not her usual talkative self. Her English teacher pulled her aside after class to ask her if anything was troubling her. "Karen, is there anything that you would like to talk to me about?" Mrs. Danks asked.

"I am all right, Mrs. Danks." the girl replied, and then she burst into tears.

Mrs. Danks was a married, middle-aged mother of two girls. She immediately guessed that all was not right with Karen. She decided not to question her any further and instead sat with her until the tears subsided. Mrs. Danks decided to speak to the headmaster later.

Gail arrived to speak with Mr. Johnson and Mrs. Danks. She made notes regarding Karen's previous behaviour, grades, and social contacts. She was more than disturbed when she was told the changes, and she decided to talk to Karen's mum and dad. Her mother had taken on a night job to help with the family finances; her father took on the responsibility of looking after Karen and her younger sister, Helen. The arrangement had worked all right at first, but then he started to give Karen special cuddles when Helen went to bed. He told Karen not to tell anyone because it was their little secret. Karen was upset and told him to stop, or she else would have to tell her mum. This startled him, and he told Karen if she did that, Docs would take her away.

When Gail spoke to Karen, she said that nothing was wrong, and her dad helped her with her homework. Gail had to accept this as the truth but told Karen to keep her telephone number and ring her at any time. Karen's mum, Liz, spoke to Chris when Gail left, and he assured her that he was taking good care of both girls. Karen started to behave better at school and started to mix with her friends.

About three months passed, and then Gail answered her mobile at ten o'clock one night to hear Karen crying.

"Please come to our place, Gail. My dad wants to cuddle me again, and I don't know what to do."

"Where are you, Karen? Is Helen okay?" Gail's mind was racing.

"Helen is asleep, and Dad has been drinking beer and is having a shower. Please hurry."

"I am on my way with a police officer. Try to stay calm."

The ride only took five minutes. Chris came out of the shower wrapped in a towel—just in time to greet the police officer at the door. When he was told that she and Gail were taking the girls to a shelter for the night, he started to curse and told them that they had no right to interfere with his family.

"Our concern is for the children. You and your wife can discuss this in our office in the morning," Gail replied.

Karen ran to Gail, who told her to wake Helen and grab a few clothes. Gail bundled them into her car to take them to her home for the night. Gail made sure that one of the motel rooms was available, and Brett was waiting for them with a carer from Docs. Vera managed to calm the girls and explained that they would be all right in the morning, when their mother would come over to see them.

When Liz arrived home, Chris explained what had happened. Liz could not understand the accusations that Karen was so intent on making, however she had already made up her mind to leave the night job. Chris and Liz went to the Docs office and were told that the girls would be allowed to go home, but further meetings would be arranged in the near future.

Gail and Brett decided to go to Miska Valley at the weekend to see what progress had been made by the builders. Gail rang her parents to ask if they would like to have a lift with them. "Hi, Mum. We are going to see how the work is coming along. Do you want a lift?"

"That is a good idea, Gail. l am sure Dad will approve, How about eight?" Margaret suggested.

The framework for the main house was almost complete; it stood out with the bright green treatment for termite control. The council insisted on the treatment owing to the infestation of some gum trees and quite a few new homes in the area. The timber used was all hardwood or pine. The floor was concrete, which had to be poured as one pour so that no joins were made in the screeding a further guard against the termite. Richard had seen the devastation in a few homes around Queensland.

Margaret had noticed a round ball about the size of a soccer ball hanging very high from a tree, ands when she asked the builder what it was, he told her to get a pest inspector to have a look at it. The inspector, Hugh, told her that it was a termite nest. He asked Richard to build a small fire and, when it was very hot, to make a nest in the middle. He cut the branch that was holding the nest and carried it very carefully to the fire. The little white insects with the orange heads tried to crawl out but were burnt very quickly. Hugh explained that the termites moved underground, mostly along mud trails that they built as they went looking for soft timber to eat. Gail and Brett were fascinated by the life of the white insect and decided to look on the Internet when they got home. Hugh also explained that the humble ant could develop wings during summer and fly in swarms, looking for new territory to invade.

Brett was very concerned and asked them if they were sure that they wanted to live at Miska Valley.

"Yes, Brett. We have done the research, and Hugh has been very helpful." Hugh carried out a thorough search of the property and was going to spray every year. Arsenic baits could be placed and inspected regularly. The ladies felt that they needed a cup of tea after all the termite talk. Margaret put the rug on a grassy patch, and they enjoyed the little cakes that Gail had brought along. Margaret poured the coffee and tea, and she said, "We can have an inspection of the framework now." Richard had been adamant that no steps were needed to gain access to the house, so low ramps had been built at the front and back leading from the both patios. The two bedrooms were near the front of the house and were quite large with an en suite for each room, one with a bath and shower and the second with no bath. They would both have lovely vanities and toilets. The kitchen area was not too large, and the laundry was large enough for two. The dining, lounge, and family rooms looked spacious. Plenty of windows provided a view of all the acreage, especially the lake.

They decided to go for a walk through the bush and try to name the various trees. "We will have to buy a book and little tags so that we can remember all the names," Margaret said.

"I know what I will buy you for Christmas, Mum," replied Gail.

One of their neighbours waved, and Richard beckoned for them to come over. He was a tall man of about seventy with a thick crop of white hair and an obvious tan from the sun.

"Hello. My name is Richard, and this is my wife, Margaret, and daughter and son-in-law, Gail and Brett."

"Glad to meet you. My name is Peter. We have been here about eighteen months and love it." Peter went on to explain that his wife's name was Denise, and they had three children who visited now and again. He had retired a few years ago from owning a motor repair business, and he found that living by the lake without all the noise was paradise to them. "We have a Labrador bitch we call Sally, and two little kittens, Mandy and Dusty. They are all spayed and micro chipped, and they stay pretty close to home."

"Do you fish on the lake, Peter?" asked Richard.

"Yes, we do. You will have to come over one day when you move in, and we will have a good talk."

Peter said good-bye when Sally came looking for him. The family gathered up a rug and piled into the car. Brett and Gail were very impressed with the building so far; they discussed tiles and carpets and, more important, roof tiles and bricks. The time flew past, and then they dropped off the parents and arrived at home just in time to welcome David from the school bus.

"How was school today, David?"

"Good, thank you, Dad. I have a new assignment to work on for the end of the month."

"What is the theme?"

"The Anzac Story Sir says that we should never forget our military men and women, who fought to save our freedom."

David had a drink and biscuit, and then he went to the computer to research the Anzacs. *This will take a while,* he thought to himself. He had made a few notes when his mobile rang: it was his friend Mark from soccer, asking him to go to the park for a kick around. *That is more fun. The Anzacs can wait.*

Gail and Brett spent some time talking about the termite situation. Brett said, "The environment is certainly changing, and the pests are out in the country building huge mounds and eating the discarded timber. Now we humans are moving into their environment. We as humans have a lot to answer for."

Gail agreed and noted, "Peter was very friendly. I hope Denise will be a good friend for Mum, and I hope Mum and Dad get a cat and dog too. They will most likely share the duties of boarding each other's animals when holiday times come around." She paused and then said, "We haven't heard from Sandy for a while. Now that she has moved into the new house at Manly and her mum has moved in too, it will be a lot easier for her to get a part-time job. We will have to go over to Manly to see the new house and say hello to Pam. From what Andrew says, she has had a pretty rough life, losing three husbands in sad circumstances. Christie, Jason, and Scott love Goldie and Pebbles, and I am sure that Pam will keep an eye on them when Sandy starts work. Christie is growing into a beautiful teenager. I hope that she can concentrate on her studies and make something of herself. Andrew needs to put his foot down; you can't just assume that life goes on, especially now the boys are showing a lot of interest. I believe that Christie has one boyfriend. Andrew and Sandy need to arrange outings for all of them and the boyfriend. I have seen so many girls deciding to become pregnant for what they think is an easy life, living on welfare or marrying someone with a little in the bank. They need to find a career that will satisfy them and then find a partner. I cannot push my ideas onto either of them, but I have seen so much wasted talent in the young girls whom I help. I will try to talk to Christie in a grown-up manner and see if that helps. I will ring Sandy tomorrow to ask if we may come to see her and the new house."

They took David over to see Andrew and Sandy. The twins were very pleased to see David, and they introduced him to Goldie and Pebbles. Then they all had a swim in the lovely, cool water of the pool.

Chapter Six

‐‐‐❦‐‐‐

S andy decided to search the local papers to find a part-time position that would fit in with both her mother and her lifestyle. She knew that her mother was planning travelling with her friend Betty. Sandy applied for the position of account manager for three clients of Louisa Cosmetics, and she hoped that it would ease the restlessness that plagued her. When she told Andrew about the position, he was happy for her but was a little apprehensive, knowing that she would have to attend conferences from time to time. Sandy explained to the three children that short absences would be necessary as part of her job; Pam would be there to take care of all their needs on those occasions.

Sandy had been with the company for about six weeks when she was told to attend her first conference: three days at Hervey Bay in a five-star hotel. Andrew made sure that her car was checked for the drive, and he arranged to take her out to dinner at their favourite seafood restaurant the night before. Sandy set out for Hervey Bay with a light heart. She was very sure of Andrew's love and knew that Pam would look after the children.

All the salespeople were escorted to their rooms and were instructed to report to the bar area for a get-together and a quiet drink. They were then asked to adjourn to the conference room and make themselves comfortable for the beginning of the lectures.

Sandy noticed Glenn's beautiful, shiny dark hair: it had a slight wave that drooped a little over his left eyebrow. Glenn's blue eyes looked at her with a lustrous twinkle in them. The conference progressed in the usual manner, with demonstrations and whiteboard questions and answers.

When the lunch break began, Glenn noticed a vacant chair next to the tall blonde, and he very quickly sat down and started a conversation with her. "How are you finding the conference so far?" he asked.

"Very interesting The trainers do come up with some comical ways to help push the products," Sandy replied.

"Yes, that is true. Which type of products are you interested in?"

"I work for Louisa Cosmetics. I feel that they have come up with some new, helpful products for our skin."

"That is interesting. My line is shampoos and hair products. May I ask your name?"

"My name is Sandy. What is your name, sexy?"

"Glenn," he replied.

They enjoyed a very pleasant meal, a glass of wine, and a lot of jovial conversation with fellow sales people. The participants seemed to be about half and half in terms of male and female. The talk was mainly about customers who liked to argue about products. Sandy could feel the vibes between herself and Glenn, and she slipped off her left shoe and gently rubbed her stockinged foot up and down Glenn's ankle. *I think the night will be interesting,* thought Glenn.

Sandy had chosen a deep royal blue ensemble with a feminine pale blue blouse. She did stand out from most of the other women, whose choices were mainly black with rather stiff white blouses. They had all been asked to pin their gold name badges onto their jackets, but Sandy preferred to put her badge in her pocket. A very nice dinner of three courses was spread on the long tables in the dining room; the barramundi followed an entree of oysters and a small salad. When the dessert of crème caramel was served, Sandy passed her plate to Glenn. "That is enough for me. The dessert looks delicious, but I would rather you eat it," she said.

The tables were placed in groups of six, which made the conversation very easy to follow. It was mainly about the day's proceedings and a little about the companies where they worked. Sandy learnt that Glenn worked for a company in Tweed Heads. It was well after ten when the groups started to break up for the night. Surprisingly, Glenn walked Sandy to the lift (he was thinking of his family at home) gave her hand a gentle squeeze, and said that he would see her in the morning. She was feeling very tired after the long drive and concentrating on the information from the seminar. She made some notes to help her give a good report to her boss on Monday. After having a lovely warm shower and putting on her pale mauve pyjamas, she crawled into bed and thought about Glenn. *I bet he knows how to please a woman.* She smiled to herself as she drifted off to sleep.

When Glenn woke in the morning, his first thoughts were about Sandy, but he knew that she would be trouble if he let things get out of control. He decided to ring his wife, Carol, to tell her about the conference so far. He finished by saying that he missed her and made a date to take her out to dinner on Saturday night.

Sandy rang Andrew, but he had already left for work, so she spoke to her mother and Christie. Sandy gave them her love and said that she would see them on Friday.

Sandy greeted Glenn with a very welcoming smile when she entered the conference room. She had slept well and asked Glenn if he had as well.

"Yes, thank you, Sandy. I think all the wine went to my head."

"The hotel is really lovely. I will go on a little tour after our time today. Do you want to come with me, Glenn?" Sandy wanted some alone time with him.

Glenn could read the signs. "Thank you, Sandy. I will think about your invitation."

All the salespeople were given positions either in a phantom company or as irate customers, in order to learn how different situations could arise. The session was a lot of fun, and the presenters made sure that a few lessons were learnt during the debating time that followed. Sandy made sure that she sat next to Glenn during the lunch and dinner breaks; they both joined in the fun and expectations of the whole conference.

The dinner on day two was a baked leg of lamb with a selection of roast potatoes and other vegetables. The entree consisted of a light cheese and tomato dish. Sandy decided to miss the entree and have some of the lemon meringue pie for sweets. Coffee and tea were served with small peppermint chocolates. The host for the conference stood up and said that she hoped that they would all take quite a lot of helpful hints back to their workplace to use in the future. A round of applause burst forth in appreciation of the presenters' hard work.

Sandy waited for Glenn by the pool, and the two of them started to wander around the beautiful gardens. Some of the guests had left to go home, and the remainder went to their rooms for an early night to prepare for the drive home early the next morning. When they approached the door to Sandy's room, she quickly glanced each way to make sure that the corridor was clear. Then she opened the door and took Glenn's hand to pull him inside. After closing the door, she slid her arms around his neck and planted a kiss on his lips.

Glenn put his hands on her elbows to ease her onto the couch and said, "Sandy, we should not be doing this. I have a wife and three children waiting for me at home."

"Don't worry, Glenn. I am in the same position, so we will have to keep it a secret between us."

They sat talking for some time until Sandy became impatient and decided to unbutton his shirt and caress his chest. She threw the shirt aside and started to remove her blouse. She pushed him onto his back and climbed on top of him. His resolve to stay strong disappeared when he found his face pressed against her bare breasts.

"Oh, Sandy, you are a little devil. I can't resist you! Your hands are like silk, the way that you are caressing me."

"How about we share a shower and jump into the bed?" she purred

Glenn loved Carol, but he had never had the feelings in his body that he felt now. Sandy rubbed him all over with sweet-smelling soap and invited him to do the same to her. They used fresh, fluffy white towels to dry their bodies, and then they crawled into the queen-sized bed to satisfy each other again.

"I should have made sure about contraceptives earlier, Sandy."

"All taken care of my sweet I have no intention of jeopardise my marriage."

When they woke, the sun was creeping around the curtains. They made love again and then proceeded to get showered and dressed for breakfast in the dining room. Glenn returned to his room to check that he had everything in his bag, and then he met Sandy before driving home. There were six people in the dining area, and Sandy approached their table. She sat down after greeting them and looked at the menu. The conversation was all about the seminar and the benefits it would be to their various jobs. Some of the men indulged in a cooked breakfast of steak, eggs, and bacon; the ladies decided on the continental instead. Everyone agreed that the venue was excellent. They spoke about their destinations and decided that the time had come to say farewell. Sandy shook hands with everyone and walked to her car for the drive home.

She had exchanged telephone numbers with Glenn earlier in the morning and decided to hide the scrap of paper with the number printed on it in her car for the time being. She thought about Glenn a lot while she was driving. She had enjoyed his company so much, however she knew that their affair had to be kept under wraps so that neither family would find out. Andrew was still a great lover, but he was always preoccupied with his work, so it wouldn't hurt to have a little fling on the side. *We will have to be very discreet.*

Her mind turned to the children and Pam. She must ask her mother if she had made arrangements for a trip with Betty. The boys' soccer game was on Sunday as usual, and Christie's tennis game was on Saturday. Sandy arrived home just as the children were walking down the street.

"Hi, Mum. Did you have a good trip?" asked Jason

"Yes, thank you. It was very educational, and the hotel was beautiful."

"Nana told us that she is going on a trip with Betty to New Zealand soon. She said that she had to talk to you about the arrangements," Christie told her mother.

"Thank you, Christie. We will discuss it later."

The children all had homework to fit in with their sports, and Andrew was at work. As usual Sandy had plenty of time on her hands, so she emptied her suitcase and put her clothes away. She took steak out of the freezer and peeled and washed the vegetables. Her mind kept wandering to Hervey Bay, Glenn's dark hair, and the very enthusiastic love making they'd enjoyed. *I wonder when I will see him again.*

When Andrew arrived home, she made sure that she greeted him with a big hug and a kiss, and she told him how she had missed him. She had changed into a loose-fitting top and shorts so that his hands rubbed her back and breasts.

"Sandy, I have been very busy at work, but I have missed you too."

"We will have to make up for the three days when we go to bed," she said.

Pam asked Sandy if they could talk about her trip, but she asked her mother if they could discuss it over the weekend. When the children went to bed, Sandy curled up to Andrew on the couch. He didn't appear to want to talk about her trip, which was what she wanted.

Chapter Seven

*D*enise and Peter were working in their garden when Richard and Margaret drove onto the property. Peter called out to them to come over for a cuppa after they unloaded the car. Sally joined her master with a friendly tail wagging.

"This is a nice surprise for the two of you to arrive at this time," they joined their hosts on the patio to look at the shimmering lake's small ripples glistening in the sunlight. The very trendy table and chairs were set up with lovely china from a bygone era. Denise pointed out to Margaret that she was not replacing her lovely dinner sets with the modern plain white, which was so popular with young couples at the moment. The cloth had some beautiful birds embroidered on each corner and a lot of greenery, which made the birds appear to come alive. Mandy and Dusty were chasing each other in and out of a large cardboard box that Denise had placed at the end of the terrace.

Richard told them that they were going to buy two kittens when the house was ready, because they could be so much fun to watch. "We will be like you and lock them up at night, to help protect the wildlife."

"The cloth is beautiful, Denise. Did you do all the work?" Margaret asked.

"Yes. I guess fancywork has been replaced by iPods these days, but I still enjoy cross-stitch How about you, Margaret?"

Margaret explained that she had become a little rusty owing to helping run the furniture business, however her desire for handicraft was still there.

"We have a local Baptist church, and the ladies run a craft morning each Friday. I go sometimes. How about you join me?"

Denise was a very active lady in her sixties. She had salt-and-pepper colouring in her short, well-styled hair, as well as green eyes and light tanned skin that she protected with a large-brimmed hat. She said that she enjoyed the rides on the boat but looked forward to the two men spending time fishing so that she could spend her time doing more homely activities.

"I would be very happy to go to classes with you, Denise. I would love to try my hand at oil painting once more." Margaret was excited at the idea.

The men had returned after Peter showed Richard his fishing boat. "We will go for a cruise around the lake after morning tea. The ladies might like to come too."

The freshly baked scones and spread with jam and cream, which Denise put on the table, were delicious. Peter and Richard carried on their conversation about the good and bad points of various boats.

"My boat is a Why Ray 195 Sport 2500 model. I bought it about two months ago, and Denise loves it too." Richard noted that a black band on the sides had a red and white trim, and there were two bucket seats with further seats behind, which would be ideal for a few passengers. The two electric outboard motors sat neatly on the back of the boat. Peter had a small wharf with a runway into the lake for easy access. When the morning tea was finished and cleared away, the four of them went to the little jetty to board the boat. Peter whistled at Sally to join them. Peter reminded them that they must put their life jackets on before boarding the boat. Margaret and Denise sat in the rear, and Richard sat near Peter to see him start the motor. The boat started with a subtle gurgle and then sped out onto the water with a large wave following behind. Peter steered the boat down the length of the lake and then swung around for the return journey.

Margaret said, "This is so very relaxing, Richard. We will have to go to the boat shop and choose one."

Peter handed the steering over to Richard so that he could feel confident when he tested the boats on sale. Richard's reaction was a little wobbly to start with, but it didn't take long to get the hang of it. Peter appeared to be very capable at handling all the aspects; he told Richard that he had had a lot of experience when he was working with the maritime services. Peter was involved with both electrical and plumbing trades during his life, and he found both skills to be a great advantage. Peter took the boat into a little grassy area that looked as if it had been mowed; the little beach in front was covered with almost white sand, which made it easy to pull the boat safely to shore. They got out, spread two travel rugs on the soft grass, and sat and surveyed the scenery. Sally jumped out of the boat to follow the men into the small, winding tracks that could be seen trailing into the bushes.

"Have you walked down the tracks, Denise?" asked Margaret.

"Yes, we have ventured a few times, but you have to keep your eyes peeled for any sudden movement. Snakes have been known to frequent the scrub. However, if you don't annoy them, they will usually slither away."

Margaret took the camera out of her bag and decided to take a few snaps so that she could show the children next time they came to visit. Some of the little clumps of bushes had very small, beautiful flowers and red and green leaves on display. *I really will have to buy a few books on native plants,* Margaret thought.

The men wandered down a track, and the ladies decided to sit on the rugs and marvel at the peace and quiet that lay before them. "Just to think of the years that we spent racing in and out of traffic and shopping centres this must be close to paradise, Denise?"

"Yes, Margaret. Some of our friends didn't make it to retirement."

Margaret told Denise that she had raised two children, and that both children were married with families. Denise was very enthusiastic about her own family and said that they had three children. Her daughter, Keiran, and the youngest boy, Paul, were married; the eldest boy, Chad, was still fancy free. Chad did a lot of travelling for his work and didn't want to be tied down yet. Peter and Denise were the proud grandparents of four little ones: Ruby, Maddie, and Emma, and one six-year-old boy, Cooper.

"We love them all and enjoy it when they come to visit, but I must admit it is good to see them leave again," Denise said.

"Our three are a little older, but I am looking forward to moving here for the same reasons as you."

When Peter and Richard came into the clearing, they were talking about fishing. *That sounds interesting,* thought Margaret. Peter was telling Richard about an association that was excellent for getting information; he said that he had joined up and suggested that Richard do likewise. Peter explained that a fishing permit had to be obtained from the local rangers. Margaret spotted a few fish swimming past the little beach. The sunshine made the silver flash as they darted here and there. The authorities took good care of the recreational fisherman to make sure that only boats with electric outboards used the lakes. Camping grounds were not permitted around the lake, and waste baskets were placed here and there and emptied at regular intervals.

"What fish can be found in the lake, Peter?"

"The lake is stocked by the Recreational Fishing Enhancement Program, which is controlled by the government. Golden perch, silver perch, sarataga, Mary River cod and Australian bass can be hooked at different times. The breeding system was introduced some years ago, and nature carried on. Fly fishing is easy because many fish are prone to surface feeding." A discussion followed between the four of them as to which fish they preferred. Margaret had had very little experience in the gutting and cleaning of the fish, and her previous fish eating had started with the local fish shop. Denise assured her that she would help to get her started on this rather unpleasant job.

The rugs were rolled up and put into big plastic bags so that they would not get splashed by the wash of the boat. Peter completed the tour of the lake and then returned to the little jetty.

"Thank you so very much. You have made us so keen to move here as soon as possible," Richard told them.

Margaret and Richard carried on with their inspection of the builders' work and went for a walk along the driveway to decide which trees they would like to plant. Margaret thought deciduous was best so that they could have sun in the winter and shade in the summer. "I want to plant an oak tree, an Illawarra flame tree, and a Jacaranda, among many others."

"We don't want a botanic garden, Margaret."

"Why Not!" Margaret exclaimed

The light-hearted argument carried on for some time until they decided to head back to Brisbane. The swimming pool was almost ready to have the water poured in. The safety fence would have to be installed first, and this was to be black aluminium with a locked, childproof gate. They had been looking at suitable small shrubs for the pool and thought that the time was right to buy them so that they could be put in place next time. "We will have to buy some comfortable lounges and umbrellas to place around the pool, Richard."

"Yes. It will be too hot to sit there in the sun."

The large pavers had been laid around the pool in a dog bone pattern; it was very attractive and made the area look bigger.

The children would love to spend their holidays here at the guest house, which was spacious enough for short breaks. The bunk beds would be ideal for the boys, and the pretty single bed would work for Christy. Margaret said, "I will go to Spotlight and choose the donnas', mattresses, and sheets for all the beds. I'll ask them to deliver in a month or two."

Margaret and Richard were feeling very light-hearted when they packed up to head back to Brisbane. Andrew had left a message on the phone regarding Sandy's mother planning a trip to New Zealand. He asked whether Margaret could stand in as a babysitter if Sandy had to work while Pam was away.

Margaret replied that she would be available to help out if needed. "I guess Pam will only be travelling for a couple of weeks. I will check with Sandy to ask what her arrangements are."

Richard was a little concerned and reminded her that they had a lot to arrange for the big move to Miska Valley.

"Christie might like to help me choose the furnishings for the guest house. I think her favourite colour is mauve," Margaret replied.

Richard decided that he would be happy with any colours they chose, but he said that he thought very light shades were best. Margaret was enthusiastic about her decision to involve Christie and was looking forward to talking to Sandy about it.

When Margaret got home, she told Gail about her plan to involve Christie. Gail thought that Christie would be thrilled. Margaret rang Sandy to tell her about involving Christie with the furnishings and asked her to arrange a suitable time for Christie to go to Spotlight with her. Christie liked the idea and suggested any Sunday that suited Margaret.

Chapter Eight

S andy arranged to talk to Pam about her and Betty's trip to New Zealand. They decided to sail on the P&O cruise ship around the main ports in Australia, and then they would land in Auckland and travel by coach around the north island first and then the south island. The trip would take about one month, and then they would fly home.

Sandy told Pam that Margaret had agreed to look after the children if Sandy had to go on a conference for her work. Pam had bought some glamorous clothes in the hope that she would meet up with a rich widower once more. Betty had accompanied Pam on her shopping trips; her taste in clothes was a bit more conservative, with subtle mauves and pinks. Pam had found a beautiful mohair shawl in a sapphire blue that managed to cover most of her private parts with a sexy allure to her ample bosom. She had bought two pairs of white slacks and one of black; they were both slim line, which showed her hip line to perfection. Both women had purchased three or four tops that enhanced their curves to be obvious to any observer. Pam showed them to Sandy for approval.

Sandy thought that her mother had not lost her talent for attracting attention. "You had better not show any of your garments to Andrew, Mum. He thinks that you are a grandma, not a siren!."

Pam laughed at her remark and reminded Sandy, "The only way to get what you want is to flaunt it. Don't let any man take you for granted, my darling daughter."

The two women managed to fill two suitcases each, and they also had a small carry-on case each. When all the travel documents were paid for and put into secure wallets, their spirits were very high. The boarding time for the trip was 7:00 a.m. on Thursday.

Pam decided to cook a lovely baked dinner for the family on Wednesday evening; it was enjoyed by all, and the children promised to take good care of the animals while she was away. When Andrew saw Pam ready to go on her trip, he remarked that she looked a million dollars. She had chosen her black slacks, black high heels, and a black-and-white blouse with tiny red markings and a large sash. Her blonde hair was held back with a small bandana, and her make-up was very well applied.

Andrew loaded all the cases into the boot of his car and went to pick up Betty. Betty was very excited and looked smart in her mauve top and black slacks. Her hair and make-up were neat and attractive, and Andrew was struck at the stark difference between the two friends. Sandy slipped into the front seat, and Pam climbed into the rear with Betty. Sandy had given the children strict instructions to finishing to get ready for school. The children had said their good-byes to Pam and expected their parents home within the hour.

On the cruise, Pam and Betty shared a cabin that had a porthole; it was on a high level, which made the sea look a long way down. They decided to put their clothes in the drawers and then explore the decks. The deck chairs were arranged around the swimming pool, which looked very inviting.

"Do you feel like having a swim, Betty?" Pam asked. She was dying to try her costume out in the clear blue water.

"Okay, Pam. It is very hot in our slacks." They had both chosen one-piece costumes with cut-out designs. Betty was in blue, and Pam had a light gold with sea motif in mainly green and blue. They both had a desirable tan on their legs and backs.

"This is lovely, floating around without a care in the world. I'm glad that we have the bathing caps to cover our hair."

"Yes, Pam, my hair does take quite a while to dry, but the swim is worth it."

"I am starting to feel peckish. I will meet you in the cabin."

They took their time to have a shower and put on cotton dresses that showed their legs off, with smart sandals on their feet. They selected a light chicken salad for lunch. The table was laden with all types of tempting dishes, but they decided to keep to their resolve of staying slim. The deck chairs were inviting, so they both settled down with some of the many brochures to read. A few glasses of wine followed. The sunshine and the gentle swaying of the ship soon closed their eyes, and they took a short nap.

They both woke with a start when a deep voice inquired if they would like some company. "Hello, my name is Fred. Do you feel like another glass of wine? We couldn't help noticing two lovely girls sitting all alone."

"Hello, Fred. My name is Pam, and my friend is Betty. Thank you for the offer."

The waiter was beckoned, Fred introduced his companion as Tom, and the four of them settled down to an enjoyable chatter. They discussed the trip and agreed to meet later in the evening for dinner, which was served in the spacious dining room. Once again the food on the menu was mouth-watering and very tempting. They all ordered salmon with salad and a few chips, Betty and Tom decided to follow on with the crème caramel. Pam was tempted but resisted.

The four of them decided to watch a movie in the well-decorated cinema. "Pam, what do you think of Tom?" Betty asked, a little concerned at his attention to her.

"He seems a very pleasant man. Just mention your grandchildren—that usually slows them down."

"Maybe he is very lonely and sees you as a homely person."

The two women excused themselves and promised to catch up in the morning by the pool. The ship steamed into Sydney Harbour, and Circular Quay and the Opera House were sparkling. The girls decided to wander around the shops, but the men decided to stay onboard.

Tom said that he would go with Betty—if she wanted him to. This alarmed Betty a little; she said that she wanted to buy some little gifts for the grandchildren, and it would be boring for him. "I will see you later in the day," she said as she waved good-bye.

Pam told her, "I think he is interested in you, Betty. If you don't want his company, just tell him."

"Pam, I do enjoy talking to him. I will have to ask some questions regarding whether he is married, and more."

"Okay, Betty. I will help you—very subtly, of course."

They enjoyed browsing around the shops so much that they decided to have a sandwich at a little cafe near David Jones instead of returning to the ship. However, time seemed to run away, and they decided to return to the ship at 2:00 p.m. Tom was so anxious to see Betty that he said that he was worried that they had got lost. His concern for her well-being touched her, and she smiled and thanked him.

"Will you both join us for dinner tonight?" asked Fred.

"Yes, we will. I think that I will have a small roast tonight," Pam answered.

During the meal, Pam started talking about her family, Sandy and Andrew, and the grandchildren. Fred told them about his family; he said that he was divorced but didn't see much of the grandchildren. Tom was more than happy to let them know that he had been widowed for two years and had one son who was married but no children as yet. He added, "I do get lonely living by myself. I have a lovely home at Manly, and I am partly retired, but I would like to have a good friend." Fred said that he wasn't looking for a permanent relationship. Pam thought that the answers were satisfactory for her, and Betty had told her that she would like to get married again if the right guy came along.

They all joined in with the dancing after the meal. The girls had put on their glamorous long dresses and the men wore suits. It was a most enjoyable evening, and Betty got a lot closer to Tom.

The next port of call was Melbourne, the home of international tennis and the Melbourne Cup. The city overall had a grey look about it, with most of the big buildings painted with grey. A trip around the city on the tram was an experience, with a short stop in the City Square. Tom was very attentive to Betty, which pleased her. Pam and Fred kept up a lot of chatter, and when it was time to board the ship, they all decided to have a swim.

Betty had been spending a lot of time studying Tom's features. His hair was pepper-and-salt and slightly receding at the front. His eyes were grey with specks of brown, and he was about six feet tall and slightly rotund. Fred was tall and slim, he had blond hair with touches of grey, and his eyes were blue. The ship had turned to head for Auckland across the Tasman Sea. Fred had started to pay more attention to Pam, but she could sense that he was a real playboy and not her type at all. She felt happy for Betty; it had been a long time since Betty's husband had passed away. The cruise was most enjoyable with lovely meals, dancing, swimming, and reading and sitting in the deck chairs. However, Auckland was approaching, and the girls' coach tour was about to start.

Pam decided to wear her white slacks and a white silk blouse to the last dance. She draped the blue mohair shawl over herself and caused a minor sensation. Fred took her hand and ushered her onto the dance floor.

The men had arranged for a hire car to drive around the two islands, and Betty hoped that they could meet up somewhere over the next two weeks, wishing that this was just the beginning. The last night on the ship was most enjoyable for the two new lovers. Tom danced all night with Betty and gave her little loving kisses. Betty had worn her favourite mauve dress with ruffled skirt and black shoes, and she'd put on her gold necklace and matching earrings to complete the outfit.

When the last dance came to an end, Tom gave her a lingering kiss and hug, and he asked her if she wanted to meet again somewhere in New Zealand. "Yes, Tom. I have enjoyed your company, and I do wish to see you again."

Tom slipped a gold bracelet on her wrist and whispered, "Till we meet again." They exchanged mobile numbers and knew that it would be a mad scramble with customs and baggage in the morning. Betty showed Pam her gift and said that she would miss him.

The next morning it was a rush to collect their baggage. Tom and Fred and left by the time the ladies' coach had pulled into the airport.

Chapter Nine

Pam and Betty were a little bewildered by all the people rushing here and there, but they saw a young lady standing with a placard with their names on it.

"Here we are, Betty. The young girl standing by the pillar is asking us to go to her."

"Now that we are on our way, we can put our suitcases on the coach."

The coach had fairly large seats with ample leg room for each passenger. The girls took advantage of the remaining seats and waited for the driver to take his seat. There were fifty passengers onboard; some had already joined at the terminal in the city. After the driver checked the number and tickets, he departed the airport. The surrounding land was very interesting, and the first stop was at a large restaurant that catered to all tastes. Pam and Betty decided on a few small sandwiches and a coffee latte. The next stop was at the motel, where they had to claim their luggage for the night's stay. All of the passengers were very quiet at this time. Betty said that she missed Tom already.

Pam said, "I hope that you can settle down to enjoy the trip, Betty. I don't want to hear you moaning all the time."

"I will try to put him in the back of my mind. I do hope that he will ring me soon."

Betty's mobile rang at eight that night. They had had a mixed seafood dish at the restaurant in the hotel and were preparing for bed. She picked up her mobile to hear Tom's voice.

"Hello, is that you, Betty? Tom here. We are staying on the North Shore tonight. We will be exploring the city tomorrow, and then we're going to the Bay of Islands. I already miss you, my love. Hope to see you soon."

"Hello, Tom. I miss you too, but we must enjoy our touring for now."

Betty went to bed happy and tried to read some of the mystery book she'd brought from home. Pam settled down to read some of her romantic novel, but the events of the day soon caught up with both of them, and they were fast asleep.

The driver asked for all passengers to meet at the breakfast area at 6:00 a.m. To start the activities, he took them around the harbour and drove them to Eden Park, where the mighty All Blacks played rugby. Some of the team were training for the big game that weekend between New Zealand and South Africa. Hamilton was the next city to arrive at for a short stopover for lunch. A lot of Maoris could be seen milling around in family groups, going on their daily chores. The city had lovely parks with a river running through the centre. The following day they travelled to Rotorua, which was about 160 kilometres from Auckland; it was very unusual in that much of it was steaming with hot springs, mud pools, and geysers. Some of the springs were volcanically warmed and were used to heat nearby buildings. It was a tourist health spot; many of the travellers had a swim in the heated baths and then got ready to enjoy a Hangi, which the local Maoris prepared for the guests. The meat and vegetables were rolled in big leaves and lowered into the ground for cooking in hot coals.

"Well, that was certainly different, Betty. Did you enjoy the meal?" Pam asked.

"Yes, I did. The smell of the sulpha when we first arrived was not very pleasant, but I soon got used to it."

The night was spent dancing and singing to mainly guitar music, which was played by good musicians. The ladies spoke to a few fellow travellers and checked the schedule for the next day.

Lake Taupo was the largest lake in New Zealand, situated between Auckland and the capital, Wellington. Tourists loved it for trout fishing. The driver drove down the side of the lake, but unfortunately he couldn't spend time fishing. A few of the travellers decided to return in the future to try their luck at fishing.

The next big stop was at the Waitomo Caves, about 200 kilometres from Auckland. The Maori had guides to help visitors into small boats to glide around the underwater lake and into the spectacular Glow Worm Grotto. The glow worms gave off an eerie blue light, and the larvae attracted small insects. While they were waiting for the bus to pick them up, Betty's mobile buzzed with a text message: "How is the trip going, looking forward to seeing you again. Love, Tom." She decided to text him later in the day.

Wellington was the next city to visit, and they spent the night in a very modern hotel that included a three-course dinner. The hotel had a modern gymnasium and a swimming pool; most of the guests enjoyed all of the facilities. Betty spent a little time deciding what to text to Tom, and then she sent her love. Pam felt that a wedding would be in the cards when they all met up again.

Sandy had sent a text to Pam to let her know that everything was okay at home. Sandy had only gone away for one night, but Andrew had managed to look after the home duties. She had arranged to spend three days at a conference next month and said that she would be ever so grateful if Pam could look after the three children. Pam decided not to tell the family about Betty's new romance—and of course she still hoped to find romance for herself before the trip was over.

Wellington was known as the windy city. It could also be very cold, and so the girls decided to wear black slacks and form-fitting blouses with light jackets. They decided to browse in the shops after breakfast, and they picked up some souvenirs to take home. Pam thought that Christie would love the shorts and bikini top with the red flowers flowing down the sides; it was harder for the boys, but she would find something sooner or later. The South Island was beckoning. Nelson was a beautiful town situated on the head of Tasman Bay, and the Nelson Lakes National Park teemed with red deer and chamois goats, which had been introduced by settlers from Europe many years ago. Pam and Betty felt as if they could spend many hours enjoying the peace of nature.

Betty had received more texts from Tom; he said that they were still near Taupo and intended to do a little fishing before they travelled further. Betty replied as usual and then hoped that his next contact would be from the South Island.

The coach was ready to leave and travel to their next town, which was Marlborough Sounds, a landlocked waterway known as Tawhitinui Beach. Pam couldn't get over the beauty of this country and how the beauty spots seemed to be so close together. They only stopped for a short time to admire the scenery and marvel at the sheep grazing on the hillside. Then the coach moved on to Blenheim, which was a beautiful, relaxed town. They spent the night there, watched a movie, and enjoyed much chatter about the many special places they had seen so far. Pam found a gentleman to talk to. He explained that his wife had died last year, and he found life was very lonely by himself. She asked a few questions, and he said that he had a lovely house in Dunedin and was heading back there now. In no time she had secured an invite to his home when she could come to New Zealand again.

The tour headed to Christchurch. The devastation of the earthquake was gradually being repaired, however the cathedral was still a mess, and many of the tourist sites no longer existed. Betty texted Tom to tell him how depressed she felt about the city. He replied and told her to keep her spirits up and to enjoy the rest of the tour. The driver took them to the repaired Avon Hotel, which they enjoyed.

The travellers were heading for Timaru, a seaside port, and then on to Aamaru. Both were lovely spots to visit. The lakes district was next on the schedule, and Queenstown was a tourist resort on the Wakatipui Lake. Betty was quite happy to wander around the town and look at the sites. Pam really let her head go with riding in the jet boats, observing bungee jumping, and water skiing. She made sure that Paul kept her company on these ventures. Paul was in his sixties and was of medium build with brown eyes and grey balding hair. They were all booked into the hotel for two nights, the meals were scrumptious, and the entertainment was exciting with dancing and plenty of music and drinking. Pam was finally in her element. She learnt that Paul had three grown children living near him in Dunedin. *I know how to handle that situation,* she thought. Betty felt that he was a very nice person and that Pam was in good hands.

Tom rang Betty to tell her that they would be arriving in Queenstown the next day. She was thrilled and rushed to tell Pam.

"We can have a double date! I guess Fred will like to come along too. The plane to Brisbane leaves about 4:00 p.m. I think Fred and Tom are booked on the same flight."

"That will be a thrill for you, Betty. Paul has asked me to go to see his house in Dunedin, but I have told him that I have to go home first."

Pam had all sorts of plans running through her head, but nothing was going to be rushed. A lovely holiday in the snow season would be great. They exchanged mobile numbers and kissed good-bye after their double date. Paul travelled home on the coach. Tom and Betty were wrapped in each other's arms; the forced separation had not done any harm. Fred was thrilled to see his friend so happy and wished them well. Betty and Pam said good-bye to all the friends whom they had met on the coach trip and said that they would keep in touch.

The flight to Brisbane was routine and took several hours. The expected time of arrival was about 9:00 p.m. Andrew had arranged with his mother to stay with the children while he went to the airport; he was a little surprised to see Betty holding hands with a strange man when they came through customs.

"Hello, Andrew and Sandy This is Tom. We met on the ship going to New Zealand."

"Hello, Tom. This is a pleasant surprise." They shook hands, and then Betty told Andrew that Fred was a friend of Tom's.

Betty and Tom arranged to meet very soon before Andrew settled the ladies in the car for the short journey home. After dropping Betty at her home, Pam said that she wasn't feeling very well. Sandy helped her out of the car while Andrew collected the bags. Pam managed to get inside and fell onto the lounge "Now mother, whatever is the matter, did you slip on the step?"

"I don't know, I just feel strange somehow, I will feel better after I rest for awhile"

Pam asked Sandy to open her large bag where she had put the children's presents, she handed them to the three children and put David's gift on the arm of the chair. The children were thrilled with the key chains and necklets with Jade sparkling on them. Christie loved the shorts and bikini top with the red flowers

"I think that I will go to my room now and freshen up." Pam was feeling giddy when she stood up.

Sandy and Margaret helped her to undress and get into bed, but her condition didn't seem to get any better. Sandy rang for an ambulance, and the medics tried very hard to save her, but she was pronounced dead, much to the distress of the children. She had had a sudden stroke.

Chapter Ten

—❦—

S andy started to panic. Margaret sat her down to calm her before the police arrived, which was necessary when a person died suddenly at home. Andrew asked his mother to make a pot of tea while he rang Betty to let her know what had happened. Betty was terribly upset and said that she was driving over straight away. Margaret told her the details, and Betty sat with Sandy to help calm her. The children heard all the commotion and wanted to know what all the noise was about. Andrew explained Pam's collapse to them.

Christie felt that Pam had let her down. "She was going to tell me about New Zealand," she said. The boys were upset and started to cry.

"Will we be having a funeral for her?" asked Scott.

Margaret managed to get the situation under control, and everybody went back to bed for the few remaining hours of the night. "We will discuss our requirements regarding the funeral and alterations to our living in the morning."

Betty drove home with a heavy heart, and she said she would ring Tom when daylight woke her.

Pam had told Sandy that she had made a will with a public trustee in Brisbane, so the funeral was the first step, which Andrew arranged with the "White Ladies." When the will was read out, a few surprises emerged. Pam had left a small percentage to her two sons, Barry and Daryl. A small amount was left to Heather and Julie, her two stepdaughters; Pam had always kept in contact with them, even if it was only at Christmas. An appropriate amount was left for Goldie to be looked after, and the three grandchildren were to have their education taken care of. Sandy was to receive the remainder of Pam estate on the condition that she handle it with care for her future.

Betty had told Tom the sad news, and he was shocked. He drove to her house and held her tight. Betty said sadly, "She was such a vivacious person, always talking and the life of the party on the ship. I can't believe it."

"Do you want me to stay over to keep you company, Betty?"

"That will help me a lot, Tom. Even though I have lived by myself since my husband died, after this shock the house seems so big and cold."

With Margaret's help, Andrew and Sandy put on a lovely memorial to Pam, mainly for family. Barry and Daryl managed to put in an appearance, and Heather and Julie said how sorry they were for the loss. Christie, Jason, and Scott had finally accepted that all people had to die someday.

Sandy was going through Pam's handbag that she had taken on the trip when her mobile rang. It was a call from Dunedin, New Zealand.

"Hello, may I help you?" Sandy answered.

"May I speak to Pam, please?"

"I am sorry, she is not here. This is her daughter, Sandy."

"My name is Paul. I met Pam on the coach tour, and we agreed to keep in touch."

"I am sorry to have to tell you that my mother had a fatal stroke the night that she arrived home."

"That is a terrible shock to you all! I am so sorry. Good-bye, and good luck. She was a lovely lady."

Sandy said good-bye and started to cry. *My mum never gave up looking for the good life.*

Tom remained at Betty's home for the next week. The romance was still very on, and Tom had taken her to see his house at Manly. "Betty would you give me the honour of becoming my wife? We could move into my home, or maybe buy a new one and furnish it to our liking."

Betty had been thinking about this possibility and couldn't see any reason for saying no. She put her arms around his neck, gave him a big kiss, and said yes. They told Sandy about their plans, and when Margaret heard, she suggested that they have a small ceremony at Miska Valley with a celebrant. In respect to Pam, they accepted Margaret and Richard's offer and decided to make the date in two months time.

Christie had been a great help to Margaret with choosing materials for the guest house: lemon with small shades of mauve and blue. The three rooms had large floor tiles in a natural shade; the small kitchen, bathroom, and laundry had smaller tiles in a darker colour. One room served as a lounge and dining room, and the other two rooms would be bedrooms when needed. Most of the furniture would be able to be folded and moved for convenience. Christie chose three large, colourful doonas, all with lemon or yellow as the main shade. She chose a plain lemon for the curtains and a brighter yellow for the cushions.

Richard and Margaret, with Gail and Brett's help, had the guest house ready. The gardener had been in to mow the surrounding grass, and the remaining work would wait until after the wedding.

Betty chose a pale blue dress with white shoes and a handbag for her wedding ensemble. Tom was in a dark navy blue suit. Tom's son stood as his best man, and Sandy stood as the maid of honour. The ceremony was sweet and short, and then they all settled down to a long afternoon tea. When the newlyweds departed, Margaret took them all on a tour of their soon to be new retirement home. Margaret said it was a shame that Pam never saw it; she was going to come here when she came back from New Zealand. The three boys enjoyed running through the trees as usual and looking at the rooms in the guest house. Gail and Sandy thought that Christie had done an excellent choice on the colour scheme. The large house was almost finished, but Margaret and Richard would have to visit Spotlight again for more ideas. The new furniture was all white and was ordered to be delivered next month. The garden furniture was mainly green and bright colours for furniture around the pool. The aluminium pool fence was due to be installed shortly with the childproof gate.

Sandy had been thinking about her work situation now that Pam was gone. She spoke to Margaret when she was alone and out of Richard's hearing. "Margaret, you will have to stay over at my place while I am at my three-day conference in Noosa next month."

"Sandy, we are almost ready to move here. I can't expect Richard to handle everything on his own."

"Well, I can't put it off because I may lose my job."

"You can talk it over with Andrew, but you said that you would do it when Pam was due to be away."

"Yes, Sandy, but things are a little different now."

Margaret sighed. "I will talk to Richard and let you know."

Sandy had to be content with that answer at the moment however she was not going to say no to her trip to Noosa. She found it hard to attend to all the functions that Pam had managed for her, such as supervising homework and making sure that the children got to practises on time.

Andrew understood that working was Sandy's outlet. Even though it was only part-time, it had made her a far happier person. He decided to have a talk with his parents to work out a solution. Margaret decided that the move to Miska Valley could be delayed for a month, but Richard was worried that Sandy would be telling them how to run their lives.

The retirement home was looking fantastic. The walls were all rendered in a pale sand colour with a biscuit shade on the eves and guttering with white window frames and a darker biscuit colour on all the doors. The main front door was almost all frosted glass with a polished timber in the middle. The patios were large, sand-coloured pavers with awnings of aluminium to keep the afternoon sun at bay. The swimming pool glistened in the sun and looked most inviting. The pool furniture consisted of two lounge chairs and two portable chairs; a few blow-up toys sat ready for play time. The lawn around the house was green and lush with bright, hardy plants; Margaret hoped that she would not have to do too much gardening.

They invited Peter and Denise over to have a look and told them that the furniture would be gradually moved in over the next month. The neighbours had Sally with them, and she seemed to approve of everything. Margaret told them about Sandy's mother dying suddenly and about their dilemma regarding the three grandchildren. They drove back to Gail and Brett's motel, and Richard spent a lot of time talking to David about his assignment on the Anzacs. David was enjoying his studies, and his results were proving to be more than satisfactory. Gail spent quite a lot of time helping with his homework and searching out information for him to read. He still found time to play footie and mingle with his school friends. Brett also found work for him around the motel, which he felt it would help him as he approached adulthood.

Gail was still very busy with her child protection work. There were not enough case workers to check on the 16,500 neglected children in NSW, and when children were removed from their homes, the necessary steps were not in place to make sure that other children were not at risk in that home. When it was a case of sexual abuse, and the father often married a new partner, he'd have a child and the problem started all over again. Caseworkers only visited the child at home if a report had come in. Sometimes the mother has a hidden dislike of her own child, which could make it very hard for a care worker to understand and then help both mother and child. Community services did not keep an account on how many siblings an out-of-home care child had living at home.

There appeared to be more babies being abandoned, whether they were being left on strangers' doorsteps, at bus stops, or even being left to die somewhere. Gail became upset at times, and she was grateful that Brett was there for her at these times. They had often thought of selling the motel, but as Brett said, it was their way of helping to protect the vulnerable children until a foster home was found for them.

Margaret and Richard enjoyed sharing their lifestyle with Gail for a short while, however the time had come for the big move to Miska Valley. "We can buy a golden retriever puppy and a couple of playful kittens to keep us amused," said Margaret.

"Yes. We will name the retriever Heidi, and the kittens will be named later."

A kennel had to be purchased for the dog, with a soft, washable mattress, eating and drinking bowls, and shampoo to keep Heidi well washed because she would be inside quite a lot. The kittens would be living mainly inside to protect the outside environment. A leash was another important purchase for Richard to consider; he could take Heidi for long walks in the bush. He told Margaret, "And I am sure that she will love to swim in the lake when we buy our boat."

"I am looking forward to our move, Richard. When I think back on all the hard work that we managed in our furniture business, it was well worth it."

"Yes, Margaret, we have earned our retirement. We will have some lovely trips overseas as well."

Chapter Eleven

Margaret agreed to stay at Andrew and Sandy's home so that Sandy could attend the conference in Noosa. Richard was not pleased; he was concerned for Sandy but felt that she should be content to stay at home more and focus on the children's education, like Gail did.

"I believe that Pam left her quite a bit of money in her will. Why does she have to go away on conferences?" Richard said to Margaret.

"I think it is just her restless nature and the type of work that she prefers."

"Let her find a more suitable job, if she has to work outside the home." Richard was annoyed.

Margaret kept her word and took a small overnight bag to stay with the children. Sandy had bought a new car with some of the money that Pam had left her, and she put her bags into the vehicle and prepared to leave in the morning. She went into the two bedrooms to give each child a kiss and special hug before settling herself in the new Astra. It was white with black upholstery, and Christie thought it was very swish.

"Can I learn to drive it, Mum?" she asked.

"When you are a little older" Sandy acknowledged that that day would come soon enough. *Time just seems to run away. I hope that*

Margaret can manage the homework. It has been a while since Gail and Andrew went to school. The traffic was starting to get heavier as Sandy headed north, and the rain had started again. The car was behaving well and was a real pleasure to drive. She started to think about Glenn. They had not spoken since the last time that they'd seen each other because they agreed that the risk was too great. The hotel that was holding the conference was on a main road and should be easy to find, with its light shades of pink and grey and very large palm trees along the front. Sandy had chosen the same blue blouse with a white skirt and white high heel shoes. She had a black attaché case on the back seat that held all her necessary notes and brochures for the lectures.

Sandy pulled into the parking space between two other cars and pushed the button to open her boot. To her great pleasure Glenn appeared from nowhere and removed her suitcase.

"This is a very pleasant surprise, Glenn."

"I was hoping that you would be coming, Sandy."

"I have a lot to tell you. Do you like my new car?"

They proceeded to the reception to book their rooms, and Sandy told Glenn about losing her mother to a sudden stroke and about her mother-in-law agreeing to look after the children for the three days. She explained that the arrangements were only temporary because her father-in-law was not happy. They were poised to make the move to their retirement house at Miska Valley, and Margaret had agreed to hold off until Sandy had returned.

Sandy had a room next to another girl whom she had met at a previous conference, and Glenn was booked into a room around the corner. *Thank goodness for mobile phones,* she thought. Sandy buzzed Glenn to say that she would be there in ten minutes. They knew that they would have to be extra careful because everybody was required to be present in the main room at 1:00 p.m. They embraced and held a lingering kiss, and then Sandy very carefully returned to her room to repair her make-up.

The participating companies presented whiteboard knowledge of their own products, which all looked and sounded very convincing; the before-and-after photos showed extra glows. The hair products featured the benefits of Argan oil; Sandy found that the oil held her blonde hair in a lovely, soft halo effect. When the meeting had a break, Glenn and Sandy made sure that they were not seen together but were not too far apart; most of the assembled people were very interesting to talk to, which made the afternoon go quickly. The dinner was salmon with a light salad and a small serving of potato chips; this was followed by stewed pears and ice cream, as well as the usual tea or coffee.

Glenn waited until he could not hear any movement in the hallway, and then he silently walked to Sandy's room. The door was not locked, as they had arranged. He locked the door behind him and checked that the safety chain was in place. He was then met by Sandy in a very pretty aqua blue teddy.

"Oh, Sandy, I was beginning to think that we would not be able to be alone."

"It has been a long time. I have missed your caresses so much," she replied.

They decided to share a warm shower, soaping each other's bodies and caressing their intimate spots. The soft white towels wiped the water away, and they rolled on to the queen size bed and kissed each other all over. Glenn had been prepared with a condom and rolled onto Sandy with ease.

"I have missed you so much, Sandy. I often think to ring you, but we made that pact not to contact each other outside of our conferences."

"I know, but it is safer this way. And absence does make the sex much better, don't you think?"

Rather than falling asleep, Glenn very reluctantly dressed and returned to his own room when they were done. They both slept well and woke in time to shower and dress for a continental breakfast.

Most of the participants ate the continental style breakfast however a few enjoyed the full bacon, steak, and eggs.

The hostess decided to select random guests to take various parts in a pretend business; this was always a lot of fun and certainly helped to relax everybody. Sandy got to know Amelia, a girl from Coffs Harbour; Amelia hadn't been to a conference before so it was all new to her. When they broke for lunch, Sandy asked Amelia to sit with her at a table for eight. Glenn and another gentleman joined them, along with another four people. The meal was light with selected cold meats and salads and cheeses.

Amelia was very talkative and chatted on about her job as a beauty consultant. She stated that she was engaged to be married in about three months. After the afternoon session, Amelia asked Sandy if she wanted to have a swim in the crystal blue pool; then she asked whether anyone else would like to accompany. *Good idea,* thought Sandy. They would all be in a group, which would keep Glenn away from her to a certain degree. The girls put on their bikinis, and most of the men wore board shorts. A lot of splashing went on, but it was nice to feel the refreshing water after such a hot day.

The evening meal was very similar to the previous night, but the sweets had changed to pavlova. The group decided to watch a movie on the television and share a nightcap. Amelia was still talking and was so wrapped up in everything that had been going on. She felt that she had learnt so many new things to do with her business. When it came time to say good night, they all left to go to their own rooms. Glenn and Sandy had agreed to meet up again after a safe period of time. The arrangement had worked last night, so they felt safe.

When Sandy heard the door close softly, she removed her clothes and threw herself into Glenn's arms. The warm shower followed, and more positions were begging to be tried. They fell into a deep sleep and were woken by the sun streaming through the window. Sandy woke Glenn and told him to wait until she dressed and left the room before he made a rush to his own room. She managed to make the breakfast call, but Glenn was a little late. Some of the guys passed snide remarks, which he did his best to ignore. Sandy sat with Amelia and let her chat away as usual; hopefully nothing more would be said about Glenn being late.

The morning session was quite serious regarding the marketing and pricing of various products. Amelia thought of ideas that she could add to her schedules. Glenn had been surprised to see how many new brands had come on to the market; he must get as much information on these products as possible. Sandy took brochures and samples to show her boss. They all decided that the three days had been well worth it.

Tea and coffee was served at 1:00 pm and the conference was officially closed so that everyone could start the drive home. Sandy and Glenn took their luggage down to the parking area, and then Glenn helped Amelia to take her bag to the car.

"You have quite a drive in front of you, Amelia," Glenn noted.

"Yes, I do, but I enjoy driving, and the weather is very good at the moment."

Glenn and Sandy had arranged to meet at a cafe in Brisbane before they said good-bye for another year or so.

"How is your family Glenn?" Sandy asked him when he arrived.

"My family seems to be managing quite well—except for me."

She told Glenn that she missed her mother's help with the children; they had really enjoyed her afternoon snacks, and she had a way of getting them to do their homework. "Mum left a lot of money for them to go to university. Andrew and I will have to guide them into subjects that will help them to have a good life in the future. Maybe Christie will be a journalist or lawyer; she likes to talk to people and find out what makes them tick. I have no idea what the boys want to study; Andrew and I will have to guide them."

Glenn seemed to think that his wife had all of the plans worked out for his children. They enjoyed a coffee each and then decided to go home. "I will see you next time, Glenn. Please do not ring me at all."

"Bye for now, my sweet. Take care, and remember to use Argan oil in your hair," he joked.

Sandy drove home to meet the children when they returned from school. Margaret met her at the front door.

"Did you have a pleasant time in Noose, Sandy? The children have been very good, and I must admit that it was good to catch up on small talk with Andrew. He does work so hard.'

"Thank you so much, Margaret. The sessions were so informative, and I met a new girl who has just started her own consultancy; she lives at Coffs Harbour."

"Richard and I would like the children to spend some time with us at Miska Valley in the school holidays, and maybe David as well."

"That will be great. The twins will enjoy David's company, and maybe you will be able to teach Christie to knit or crochet."

Sandy used to knit when she was younger, but knitting and crocheting seemed to be a dying art, which was a shame. Margaret liked the idea of teaching some of her skills to Christie. She would talk to Denise about her classes, and the three of them could go along and really enjoy themselves.

Richard was thinking about buying a Jeep Wrangler so that he could take the boys off-road driving, but this was a secret for now. *They will all spend time on the boat when we make up our minds which one to buy.* Margaret and Richard had asked Brett and Andrew if they could take their belongings to Miska Valley next week, and then the furniture would start to arrive. The next big thing was choosing the dog and kittens, domestic shorthair for the kittens(so that the fur is more contained) and a golden retriever for the dog.

Chapter Twelve

———————

*T*he big day had finally arrived. Richard and Margaret drove into the semicircular driveway to see many galahs pecking away at the grass.

Margaret said, "Oh, look at the beautiful pink and grey birds! I do hope they will stay."

"I guess we will see many more flying in and out among the trees," Richard replied.

The sight of the agapanthus around the edge of the driveway was a beautiful display of flowers, mainly blue with an occasional white head here and there. The lawn had been mown by the gardener, and the path to the main door was swept and very inviting. They drove the Subaru into the garage and took the suitcases out of the boot. The first furniture delivery was due later in the day, so they hung their clothes in the wardrobe in the main bedroom and decided to have a coffee. The sun shone in every room, and the white walls reflected a welcoming glow. The main bedroom and the lounge, dining, and family rooms looked over the lake; the remaining two bedrooms and kitchen were behind but had lovely views as well. The wardrobe doors were mirrors in the first two bedrooms, with plenty of hanging space and wire sliding drawers for easy cleaning.

The main bedroom had an en suite with a bath, shower, and a combination vanity hand basin. All the tiles were white with a small border design in light grey. The tiles were floor to ceiling, and the shower recess had glass walls and door. The guest bathroom was smaller without a bath. The kitchen was quite large with plenty of cupboard space, an electric oven, two dishwashers, and a cook top for easy meals, the bench top was mottled grey and white marble. The display cupboard had leadlight glass doors, and Margaret had ideas to put her lovely china on display there. All the floors apart from the bedrooms were large white tiles. The carpet in the bedrooms was light beige with a very pale lemon tone running through it.

A small path from the back terrace led to the guest house, which Christie had helped Margaret to decorate. The three rooms could be used as needed, the bathroom was small but adequate, and the kitchen had everything that was needed. The whole area glowed with a welcoming lemon atmosphere. The furniture for the guest house was to be all cane, for easy moving.

The furniture started to arrive in a huge van. The tradesmen carried a large three-seat lounge with two small lounge chairs, which they placed in the family room. This was followed by casual chairs and a dining suite with a glass-top table with six chairs. All the furniture was white with shades of lemon and pale green. The television was a Samsung Smart TV and fit into a corner where it could be seen from the lounge. The new mattress on the bed was a Posturepedic, which would provide many years of restful nights.

When most of the furniture had arrived, they looked around to decide what floor rugs they needed. Keeping in mind safety and warnings about loose rugs causing falls, Margaret thought that they would have to be firm. The blinds and curtains would have to be measured by a supplier as soon as possible.

"Richard, what do you think of our retirement home now?'

"I think we will be very happy here. It will be lovely to share with our children."

"We spent many years in our furniture factory, but it was all worth our hard labour. I wonder how the young couple who bought the business are coping with all the modern styles"

"We will have to go down to Banora Point to say hello sometime."

"Yes Richard a good idea."

They were both very tired after all the activity and decided to have a meal they had brought with them. Then they would have a shower and an early night. They rang both Gail and Sandy to let them know of their plans and told them how happy they were with the house.

Some strange noises through the night did disturb their sleep; possums and birds were obviously moving around, and the frogs were quite vocal.

"I wonder if the children will part with Goldie. I would like to have her here with us," Margaret said. She was a little worried.

"We can only ask them. She will love it here, I am sure."

They decided to go to the local vet to ask about adopting two kittens. As luck happened he had recently been given six little rascals to find a home for. One was nearly all white with a ginger saddle and a topknot of ginger on her head. Margaret fell in love with her immediately and named her Shannon. Richard watched a little grey and white fluffy bundle of fur racing around the floor and selected him. The vet said that they had both been fixed and would have microchips inserted when the names were decided.

"What name have you chosen, Richard?" asked the vet.

"I think he looks like a shadow."

"Okay, then. It is Shannon and Shadow." They laughed, paid the bill, and thanked the vet.

When they left with the instructions of what to buy to keep the little rascals happy, they couldn't wait to see whether the kittens they liked their new home. A lot of the boxes left from the new furniture were still waiting to be removed; the kittens had a great time climbing in and out of all of them and chasing each other. They ate their Friskies, drank water, and then curled up together to sleep on the lounge. Richard had bought two baskets, and he had placed near the lounge for them to curl up, but they preferred the lounge itself. "Maybe later," Margaret said, "when they get used to them."

They spread some newspaper on the floor in the laundry and put two trays with kitty litter in them; even though the kittens would be free to go outside anytime they chose only in the daylight, there was an absolute curfew at night.

Margaret's thoughts turned to the next task. "Richard, where would the best place for an herb garden?"

"I think we need to choose a small area near the kitchen that will get plenty of sun and no t too much wind. How about we go to have a look for a suitable spot?"

They built the chosen spot into a raised position with some small rocks and friable, well-drained soil with plenty of old compost. They built it up about nine inches and then put in an old metal plank for the edging. The centre piece was a dwarf Meyer lemon tree that would grow to a height of two metres. Nasturtiums would make a colourful addition among the many fragrant herbs that would be bought gradually when Margaret spotted them. Tomatoes, beans, and peas were essential, and of course thyme and oregano. Richard jokingly warned Margaret that they were only supplying food for the family, not the neighbourhood. They made enquiries at the nursery about the best way to protect the plants from insects and birds. Richard built a wire cage over the whole garden, which would also keep out the kittens.

Richard decided that he would build a bigger garden plot for the large vegetables, like lettuce, cauliflower, and spinach, but this would have to wait a while. He wanted to buy his boat and a four-wheeler first. He decided to ring Peter and Denise to ask them to have a look at all they had done so far. Peter would be able to help him decide which four wheel drive to buy. Sally trotted along next to Denise, eager to have a long walk; she had to inspect everything and then settled down for a nap on the patio.

"Hello, Denise. Do come in. We have most of the furniture in place. How about a cuppa?"

"Thank you, Margaret. We saw the furniture vans and wondered how you were coping."

Margaret took Denise through the house to each room and they inspected the burgeoning herb garden before settling down to morning tea. Denise explained how she had gradually bought more herbs and which ones were her favourites for cooking, as well as also providing pleasant odours both in the house and garden.

Peter and Richard had become very involved in the discussion about the vehicles. Peter had a red Pajero and was very happy with its performance; he said that he enjoyed off-road driving, listened to Richard talking about the Jeep, and suggested that they spend some time together with his grand children as well. Morning tea followed with talk about their respective children and grandchildren. Peter and Denise had two girls and one son. One daughter was travelling around the world, backpacking and picking up casual work at very interesting farms and restaurants. The other daughter was married with a very young boy. The son had a good teaching job at a high school in Brisbane, and they had two primary children.

Margaret and Denise spoke some more about the craft group that Denise went to each week. Margaret said, "I will be able to start going with you as soon as I can organise my wool scraps and some material that I am sure can be used for something. Do you do charity work for unfortunate people?"

"Yes, we have bundles for Red Cross and the local church."

"My daughter, Gail, works for Docs, and some of the stories she tells us are so upsetting."

By the time the men had finished the vehicle discussions, Richard had decided to buy a Jeep. Margaret decided that it was too big for her to drive, but that was okay because she had the Subaru.

Margaret introduced Shannon and Shadow to Peter and Denise; Sally was not very interested in them. Denise took two smaller boxes home for her two to play with.

"It is great to be able to spend the time watching the kittens have such fun, and to not worry about wasting time when you should be ironing or something," Margaret observed.

"Yes, retirement is great. Will you be travelling overseas for holidays?" Denise asked.

"I guess so, but we haven't settled on where to go yet. We will have to go to a travel agent after we have bought the boat and car."

When the neighbours left, Margaret and Richard decided to walk hand in hand along the foreshore of the lake, remembering their lives, all the ups and downs of the business, and Andrew's hurried marriage which had given them three lovely children.

"I often wonder what type of a girl Andrew would have chosen if he had not met Sandy," Margaret said.

"I think he would have chosen a university-trained girl. However, he has looked after the family very well, so I guess that is all we can ask for."

"Yes. Christie is a delight, and the boys will have to start thinking about their future careers."

"Christie would like to study the law, and Jason has been asking me about architecture, which is always a good career."

"Sandy does seem to have a restless nature; I guess she misses Pam a lot," Margaret said.

Richard changed the topic. "Gail and Brett seem very happy in their marriage. The motel provided a good living and a lot of help to Gail in the course of her work."

"Yes, Richard, and now we can now enjoy the many years to come—together."

"The school holidays are coming up, so we can spend a lot of time with the four children if Gail doesn't have other plans."

Chapter Thirteen

Richard and Margaret decided to have a look at four-wheel-drive vehicles. The selection was vast, and they started by looking in the advertisements in the paper.

Richard said, "I don't think that we need to buy a brand-new one, so long as the mileage is reasonable and the vehicle has been looked after."

"I am sure that the children—the boys in particular—will enjoy driving through dry creek beds and along the sand, where it is safe."

They marked a few advertisements and started to make phone calls to the sellers. Andrew and Sandy arrived with the three children and Goldie.

"She is only visiting you while we are here. We will take her home with us for now, because we would miss her too much," Sandy said. Christie clearly loved the dog.

Margaret understood why Christie didn't want to part with her beloved friend, and she decided that she would talk to Richard about buying another one.

They all wandered around to have a look at their achievements and were amazed at what they saw. Margaret told them about looking to buy a four wheeler and asked them for any advice. She said, "We would like the children to spend some time here with us in the school holidays. And what do you think of them doing some off-road driving with Richard?"

Andrew was a little hesitant. "I am sure the boys will enjoy that activity, and Christie will get a thrill which she can tell her girlfriends about."

"Gee, Pa, that would be a lot of fun," the twins said. They were very enthusiastic

Christie could think of more interesting things to do but decided to try it once or twice.

Sandy was happy to go along with any arrangements that the grandparents made; it would give her some spare time to pursue her job. She did enjoy working in cosmetics and advising customers on the best brands to use for their particular skin types. A few days away would be great too. "How do you feel about spending some time here, children?"

"That will be great, Mum. I can spend some time learning to cook some lovely cakes too," Christie said.

Andrew had a talk to them about off-road driving, telling them that they must pay attention to Richard at all times and obey all safety rules. He told them that they would have to make time to do any assignments for school and also do any chores that Nana had for them.

The next week sped past, and when they were told that David would be staying with them as well, Richard and Margaret were thrilled. Richard's thoughts returned to the business of buying the vehicle. The Jeep was still his choice, if he could find a suitable buy. Richard also decided to have a check-up with his doctor to make sure that he was fit to enjoy all these activities with the grandchildren. After many tests the doctor agreed that he was fine for his age.

Sandy spoke to her boss to let her know that she would be available if she had some more hours for her. Andrew accepted that it would be a good time for Sandy to stretch her legs and spend a little time away from household chores.

Gail thought that it would be good for David to spend some more time with his cousins, and driving in rough terrains would be a new experience for him. Gail had had a sad time lately with a young girl who had run away from a very happy home to live on the streets. It was heartbreaking to see the good parents so terribly upset to have their daughter turn her back on them. Gail spent considerable time finding her and then trying to talk sense to her, which was very hard, particularly when a layabout boyfriend was involved. When Gail found out that marijuana was involved, she decided to arrange for an intervention by a police officer friend to take her to rehabilitation in a hospital. The parents cooperated as much as they could, and the treatment started to have some good effects. Tanya decided to return to her studies and wait for a more reliable boyfriend to come along.

Margaret and Richard settled down to making more phone calls regarding the Jeep. An ad they found was from a man in Coolangatta. The Jeep was yellow and black, and the mileage was reasonable. They decided to drive over to have a look, and they asked Peter to go with them to give his opinion. Peter felt that it was a good buy. The arrangements were made: Richard and Margaret would drive the Subaru over on Wednesday and pay the bank cheque, and then Richard would drive the Jeep home. Margaret decided to have a drive around the home ground, but she said that she preferred to drive the car. Both vehicles fit into the double garage.

When it was time for the children to spend time with the grandparents, there was great excitement. Brett dropped off David and had a look at the house, garden, and the Jeep. He was most impressed. Sandy brought Christie and the boys, and they all had morning tea on the patio overlooking the lake. After Sandy and Brett said their good-byes and gave last-minute instructions to the children about behaving themselves, Margaret took Christie into the bedroom with the queen bed and asked her to put her clothes away in the cupboard. She then ushered the three boys into the third bedroom, where she had put a folding bed and instructed the boys to put their clothes into the cupboards.

"I thought that we would be sleeping in the guest house, Nana," Jason said.

"No, Jason. The house is for family. The guest house is for extra guests."

"Is there anything you want us to do for you, Nana?" Christie asked. She was always on the go.

Just then Richard walked into the room and greeted them with great enthusiasm, shaking hands with the boys and giving Christie a warm hug. "Well, now, who wants to come off-road driving with me tomorrow?"

Their faces lit up in unison, and they gave a gleeful "Yes, please." Margaret made a hamper of small sandwiches, chips, and soft drinks for them to take with them. The next decision was to decide who was going to sit in the front seat. Richard had thought of this and told them that he had four different length straws; the one who drew the shortest straw would sit in the front on the outgoing journey, and it would change on the homeward leg. He told them to get some casual jeans and tops, sturdy shoes and socks, and of course old, comfortable hats. Margaret decided to spend some time gardening and preparing the evening meal for their return later in the day.

When the children were ready for the drive, Richard told them that they were all going to play I Spy. He asked them to remember any creatures that they may spy on the drive, and when they stopped to have lunch he would give them some books to hopefully identify the animals or birds. Jason was the winner of the shortest straw, and they all climbed aboard. Richard headed for the fire trail, which led to a rugged clearing among heavy undergrowth of fallen leaves and branches. The children bounced about, with the seat belts holding them firm on the seats.

"This is a lot of fun. Are you all okay back there?" Jason said, laughing.

"Yes, I'm glad the seats are well padded," yelled Christie.

Rich growth characterised the area, with a cool green rainforest canopy that filtered the sun and resulted in a permanent twilight on the forest floor. The mottled tops of mushrooms trapped the rainwater, and python-like liana strangled the tree trunks. Very shallow creek beds meandered through the area, and Richard followed these creeks until he found a wide grass spot that he felt would be a good spot to stop and eat their sandwiches. The children managed to find the pictures of the animals that they had seen on the way in to the lovely hanging rock, which was covered with beautiful green ferns. Many tree ferns could be seen, as well as very large gum trees. The boys wanted to go exploring, but Richard said that it was not a good idea because it was too easy to get lost until they better knew the surrounding bush. Spider webs were everywhere, and some had trapped insects that were held fast with extra web wound around them. Scott was wrapped in the mechanics of the Jeep and wanted to know when he could learn to drive it. Christie had a good look at the books and read a lot of the captions while she was eating her chips.

"Do you think that we will see a snake or two Pa?" Asked Christie

"Maybe but please don't go near them if you do." replied Richard

They saw a lot of lizards scampering among the dead leaves that covered the ground. After they all finished the drinks, Richard told them to make sure that all the rubbish was in the plastic bag so that they could take it home with them. It was David's turn to sit in the front on the return journey. He enjoyed all the manoeuvres and twists and turns that Richard managed to execute, and he wanted to know when Richard would teach him how to drive. Richard said that he would start to teach them on the ride-on lawnmower around the property. He added, "Nana will be waiting for us with a lovely meal, and I guess you will have a swim before dinner."

They were very excited to tell Margaret about the very bumpy ride and all the animals they had seen. Nana had a lovely salad with fresh tomatoes and lettuce waiting when all the swimming was completed.

"Can we go driving tomorrow, Pa?" Scott asked eager to go again.

"We will spend most of the day here so that you can do odd jobs to help us, and then we will go driving on Wednesday."

Christie answered, "If you don't mind, Pa, I wish to spend time with Nana. She might like to teach me how to cook some little cakes."

They all watched some children's shows on TV and had an early night. Margaret told Richard that Denise had taken her to her craft lessons, which Margaret thoroughly enjoyed, and she learnt how to crochet bootees. Denise was busy knitting a cardigan for Peter in a very dark green, and she had agreed to copy the pattern for Margaret to knit one for Richard, if he wanted one. Richard told Margaret how much he enjoyed spending the time with the kids; they were very interesting company. They soon settled down to watch some sport on Foxtel.

"I hope Andrew and Sandy are making the most of having time to enjoy each other's company for a few days."

Andrew and Sandy enjoyed a night at their favourite seafood restaurant followed, by a movie and then a luxury night in bed. Sandy agreed to spend two nights in a conference centre in Brisbane for her company. She was disappointed when Glenn didn't attend, however Amelia turned out to be very good company, and they spent some spare time in the shopping centres. Amelia's wedding was coming up fast, and she asked Sandy if she would like to attend and to bring her husband. Sandy gave Amelia her address and her home telephone number, and she started to think about a suitable gift for them.

Chapter Fourteen

argaret decided to teach Christie how to knit. She searched through her pile of wool and found some very pretty aqua wool that would make a lovely scarf. Christie fumbled a little bit to start with, however she soon managed to twist the wool around her fingers and worked out the difference between knit and purl, and stocking stitch started to emerge. When the scarf measured about six centimetres, they stopped for a morning tea break; Nana explained that short breaks were necessary to give the fingers a rest. She told Christie that she should learn as much as possible because these activities helped to keep the mind fresh instead of playing video games.

The boys helped Richard around the outside. He had bought some small shrubs to plant in the garden near the pool fence, and the sweet smell of the fragrant gardenia would linger for some time. The green leaves always looked pretty. He decided to take the boys to the nursery to choose more shrubs to plant along the path to the guest house. They spotted some brightly coloured impatiens, which the saleswoman said were very hardy and flowered all year round.

When all the planting of the shrubs was finished, the children said that they would like to see a DVD. After a short argument, they selected on a thriller that kept them amused. The kittens soon found willing laps to settle into and started purring. Christie took up her knitting needles again when the movie was finished, and she increased the scarf by another ten centimetres. Margaret then told her to leave it for the night.

Denise came down to visit and to ask Margaret to go to her next craft session. Margaret explained that next week would be okay, when the kids went home. Denise's grandchildren only came for odd visits now and again; they were all so busy with jobs at the shopping centres in the city. Sally and Goldie chased each other around the garden and then settled down for a nap in the shade. Denise remarked how good the path to the guest house looked, with the impatiens a lovely, multicoloured showpiece. The boys told her that they had chosen the plants and helped Richard plant them.

Jason said "We are going to apply for casual positions when we turn fifteen. In the meantime, we will help Pa and learn as much as we can about looking after a home garden and maintenance."

Richard decided to go off-road driving the next morning; he told the children that they had to try to find some lizards so that they could write a short essay on their habitat and to make sketches to show their teachers. The boys piled into the Jeep, but Margaret and Christie decided to stay home with Goldie and the kittens. The men headed for the beach through the rough terrain, bumping into all the small trees and sand piles along the way.

"Oh, look at the beautiful Pelican sitting on the rock" Scott was intrigued

The Pelican was preening itself on a large rock by the shore; he keeps his plumage clean by using his bill to spread a thin layer of oil over his feathers. The oil is secreted by a gland at the base of his tail. When the pruning was completed, it soared up into the sky with its very large wings and appeared to float on an airstream. A few more pelicans joined him, which made for a spectacular air show before they all came to rest on the same rock.

Richard drove up and down the beach where nude sunbathers were resting on towels; he was trying to find a suitable place to stop. After the hamper was emptied, they ventured into the undergrowth to see what they could find. Lizards such as blue-tongued skinks had no internal mechanism for regulating their temperatures; their body heat depended almost entirely on the temperature of their surroundings, but by moving back and forth from sun to shade, or by going underground, they are able to keep their body heat within tolerable limits. Jason and Scott tried to catch one or two, but the lizards were too quick for them. David was content to watch the other two and their antics. He had been studying lizards at school and felt that their ability to survive in the blistering heat was fascinating.

The lizard dragons, range in size from a few centimetres to more than a metre. Some possess frills and ruffs that help to scare off attackers. One five-centimetre lizard may eat at least a hundred ants in one day. Many species store moisture in their skins, which helps them to survive droughts.

The seagulls were very busy salvaging by the shoreline, picking up little bits and pieces that looked enticing. Many water birds, plovers, sand pipers, and curlews were in fact waders and fed not in the waters but on the mud, sands, and reefs left exposed at low tides. Some of these birds were breeders, but most of them were migrants. They had favourite feeding grounds where they congregated in hundreds of thousands. The children were happy to sit quietly and watch them all.

Birds are the most fascinating class to watch because of the vivid colouring, though bright colouring is far from universal. A general rule is that the warmer the bird, the brighter it is, and the drier it is, the paler the bird. Two of the main functions of plumage colour are self-advertisement and self-concealment. In many species a balance is struck between these two needs; the male is brightly coloured, especially in the breeding season, and the female is camouflaged by drab colouring. This is particularly marked among the fairy wrens, whistlers, birds of paradise, and bowerbirds. The children spotted some of these birds, but as Richard explained, they usually came out later in the day.

Shy albatrosses could be seen when they climbed up onto the cliffs at the end of the beach. They crowded around fishing vessels and often approached the coast, gliding and banking low over the sea. Fish, squid and cuttlefish, crustaceans, and carrion were their food. The shy albatross is the largest of the mollymawks, approaching the wandering albatross in size. They are often seen in abundance on the east coast of Australia. David sat and watched them soar across the sky.

"Gosh, Pa, you have certainly given us plenty to think about," Scott said. He was interested in everything that he had seen and was looking forward to spending a lot more time reading about the environment. "We didn't see any whales or dolphins in the sea today. Do you think we can come another day?"

"Yes, we will come to the cliffs on your next school holiday. It is a very good spot for whale watching."

Christie spent most of the day knitting her scarf. Margaret showed her how to put the tassels on both ends, and then she searched through the wool bag to find enough wool to start knitting another scarf in red wool. Christie enjoyed the handicrafts but said that she wanted to study law when she went to university, if she manages to get a high enough mark in her higher school exams.

"Okay, young lady, you have been sitting most of the day, and your brothers will be home soon, how about a swim?" Margaret suggested.

Christie thought that was a splendid idea, and she went to change in to her bathing suit. She found Goldie's lead and then took her for a walk all the way around the perimeter of the property. She saw Denise doing some weeding in the garden and told her about the scarf that she had finished. Denise congratulated her on her first attempt and asked her if she was going to do another one. Denise had been weeding around some hibiscus bushes; one was a beautiful bright yellow with a bright red throat, and the other one was a very deep red with splashes of white on the petals. She explained that they were gross feeders that required potash every month, and they also needed to be cut back to encourage new growth for the flowers. Christie was gradually storing gardening knowledge, which she found very interesting.

The Jeep was parked in the garage, and the three boys ran over to Christie to tell her about everything they had seen at the beach.

"Get your togs on, and we can have a swim," she told them.

The water was so refreshing that they dove and splashed for an hour, until Margaret called them for another BBQ, which they enjoyed. The apple pie with fresh cream was scrumptious, and they all asked for seconds. Another game of Scrabble was organized after dinner, with more arguments over the spelling of words. It was all good fun, however, and it left them tired and ready for bed.

Andrew had seized the opportunity to arrange another lovely dinner at their favourite restaurant. Sandy always enjoyed these sojourns and made the nights very sexy. Her perfume made Andrew very heady and vulnerable. It was good to have the house to themselves because she could state her thoughts with gay abandon and leave her clothes where they fell.

The next day was spent catching up on the housework, preparing for the children to come home, and readying herself for the usual run-around of school, soccer practise, and tennis matches. The boys were doing well on their team; they played together, which was a blessing, and they both talked about joining a local cricket team. Sandy missed her mother's help with the children; they would simply have to do more for themselves. The boys were old enough to mow the lawn, and Christie could do her own washing and ironing; she could start cooking some of the meals too. It is all part of life's education. Sandy did not like being responsible for every little thing. Christie had started to show a lot of interest in some of the young boys at school, which was a worry if Sandy was not home when they got off the bus.

Gail was involved in a missing child case again. The little girl had apparently been abducted by her own father, but the mother was distraught because she thought that she could trust him to return her after the schedule visit. The police were trying all avenues with relatives and friends, but they kept coming up with false leads. Gail spent a lot of time with the young mother trying to establish why the father would take the child away from a secure environment. Did he have another girlfriend, or was he planning to leave the country given the fact that Australia was not his birth country? Gail received a tip that the child had been seen in a big department store in Sydney, and she took the mother with her to follow the lead. That path took them to a house in Enmore, and they rang the police but were told that both the father and child had gone the day before. This was frustrating for Gail and heartbreaking for the mother. Gail left Mandy in Sydney to try to contact relatives, and she flew back to Brisbane to follow up any leads that had surfaced in the last day or two. Brett said that he would pick up David at Miska Valley on Friday.

When Sandy heard about Gail's latest case, she was disgusted and said, "There she goes again, chasing after other people's kids."

When Brett picked up David, he couldn't stop talking about the great time he'd had with Pa and the cousins. He wanted to know if he could go to Miska Valley for the next school holidays.

"Maybe Nana and Pa will want to spend more time together instead of amusing you four," Brett said.

"It was wonderful having them all here," Margaret told Brett and Andrew when they were all in their vehicles.

Margaret and Richard settled down to reading holiday brochures and dreaming of what was to come. There were so many places to choose from, and they cuddled up to each other on the big lounge and dozed off.

Chapter Fifteen

Margaret spent a lot of time reading all the holiday brochures. Some trips were very expensive, and others were quite reasonable. Canada looked outstanding with the Rocky Mountains, a train journey, and a trip to British Columbia. The cruises around Italy and the European capitals looked very relaxing; not having to change accommodations all the time with heavy bags was very appealing. The more local trips to New Zealand and their own holiday spots were also beckoning. They had been tied down with their furniture business for so long the world had gone along at a very quick pace and left them behind. This was about to change, and a decision had to be made.

After talking to Andrew and Sandy about checking on the property a few times and arranging with Peter and Denise to feed the animals while they were away, Margaret and Richard decided on a trip to Europe for two months. Margaret asked Christie if she could go shopping with her to help her select some modern clothes to take. Christie was delighted, and they arranged to go on the next Saturday.

"Christie, I want you to pick a suitable garment for yourself as well, as a thank-you present."

"Thank you, Nana, but I was more than happy to help you."

The holiday was a great eye-opener for both Richard and Margaret. They managed to take heaps of photos to show the family when they returned. Margaret was not too keen on the long flights and said that she would have to have six months' break at home before they arranged another trip.

The little girl whom Gail had been trying to locate had been found by the police with her father. She had since been returned to her mother, with the father being charged with abduction. Gail decided to have a few days' stay with her mother at Miska Valley before the pair of travellers decided to take off again. Richard was very busy getting the garden beds looking good, and he had arranged for a man to clean the pool while they had been away. Gail was very impressed with the overall picture, and when she saw Denise in her garden, she decided to introduce herself. Denise told her that she had met her sister-in-law Sandy and the children.

"Sandy is a beautiful woman. She was telling me that she thinks that you spend too much time running around after other people's children."

"Sandy is a little wound up in herself, but I must admit that she is very attractive."

"She goes to a lot of conferences and seminars, she told me."

"Yes. It seems to relieve her restless nature."

"Your brother doesn't mind her going where she could be tempted to play up?"

"He goes along with most things. They want to keep a happy home life."

All this chatter intrigued Denise and cast more doubts in her mind about Sandy. The children seemed happy enough, and they obviously loved their grandparents. Gail explained how she couldn't spend as much time as she would like to with her parents because of the nature of her work.

"It must be hard on your marriage, Gail. How does your husband cope?"

"Brett is a wonderful, kind man, and we manage the motel and the disadvantaged children together."

Margaret wondered where Gail had gone, and when the three women caught up, they decided to have a coffee on the sunny patio. Sally and the two kittens joined them while Peter went looking for Richard. It was obvious to Denise that Gail had her doubts about Sandy, but Margaret thought that the sun shone out of everybody. They talked about the next trip and whether it be a sea trip or a coach one. Denise and Peter had had some very good trips around Australia and suggested that they spend some time in Sydney and Melbourne soon, perhaps for the tennis tournaments.

Richard was reading the Sunday papers when Peter found him, and Richard came across an advertisement for an adventure that would cover the entire coast of Western Australia from Perth to Darwin He thought it looked good. It was over eighteen days, and they would have to fly to Darwin and then fly back from Perth. Peter agreed that was a very good tour and said that they would enjoy it. After consulting with Margaret, he rang the travel agency and booked them for the next available tour.

Denise was sure that a current of dissatisfaction was lying under the surface of Gail's and Sandy's relationship. Denise's desire to help her friend was very strong; she would try to weed out information from Sandy, or maybe the children when next they visited. Sandy was only too happy to spend time with her; she loved to talk and tell her about the people that she met at the seminars, but she was very careful not to mention Glenn. Sandy told Denise about Amelia's wedding and said that it was a shame that Andrew had business obligations and couldn't keep her company.

Margaret asked Christie to accompany her on a shopping trip to buy light summer clothes to take to Darwin, and once more she bought Christie a lovely cotton outfit.

"Nana, you shouldn't be spending money on me!"

"But I love seeing you looking so pretty, my dear."

When all the preparations for the trip were in hand, Richard and Margaret decided to visit his old factory to see how the young couple was managing. They said that business was booming with all the new houses being built in sunny Queensland, and they took Richard and Margaret inside to have a look at what was trendy at the moment. Business was good, and they were really enjoying it all. When Richard and Margaret left the furniture factory, they went to the marine yard to look at the small runabout again. Richard said, "We will have to decide on which boat to buy when we come back from our trip to Western Australia. The fish will be plentiful, and the boys will enjoy me showing them how to manage the motor and how to bait the lines." They stopped for a light luncheon at a little cafe near the water. A small nursery was attached, and Margaret bought a few more plants and herbs.

Andrew arranged to take them to Brisbane Airport with their entire luggage on Sunday. It was exciting, and Margaret had all the necessary documents in a special bag that she carried on her hip for security.

"I see that you are well prepared, Mum. Good to see," Andrew said.

"Yes, Andrew. I found this was such a handy little bag when we went to Europe."

The three of them sat at small table after the luggage had been loaded. They had a coffee and a small cake, and then they embraced. The couple walked to the flight gate.

"Have a good trip, both of you. We will check on Miska Valley for you," Andrew said.

"Bye, love. Take care."

They found their seats and settled down to read and look at the beautiful scenery ahead. There was a lot of red land down there, with gorges and anthills spotted here and there.

The history of Darwin is fascinating. The British were concerned about the interest that was evident from the Dutch and French over the northern part of the land. The wealth of South-east Asia prompted Briton to send Captain Gordon Bremer to lay claim to the land as part of New South Wales on 20 September 1824. Because of the lack of freshwater, the soldiers moved on, and the land was declared unsuitable owing to the unbearable heat. Bremer tried again at Port Essington and named it Victoria for the British Monarch. Cyclones and mosquitoes, which were causing malaria, finally forced the area to be abandoned in 1849. Darwin was finally established in 1869 after another failed attempt; however John McDowell Stuart stirred enthusiasm in the Northern Territory and a dream of a tropical paradise. When one looks at the modern city of Darwin, it is hard to imagine the devastation after Cyclone Tracy struck on Christmas Day 1974. Darwin has come a long way since then, with many big, modern shops and restaurants. Small communities of Japanese, Indonesians, Malays, and Filipinos all have an early stake in Darwin's history; most were involved in the pearling industry.

Richard and Margaret spent four days in the city looking at the many interesting sights. Their next stop was at Katherine Gorge, with its sheer sides towering over the Katherine River; magpie geese were abundant here. Howard and Berry Springs were popular parks for sedate swimming holes with beautiful rainforest and abundant birds and wildlife.

"I am so glad that we decided to come up here, Richard. It is all so different to the countryside down south."

"Yes, Margaret. It can get very hot in Queensland, but I couldn't stand the heat up here in summer."

The coach headed to a lodge in Cicada. They had been told not to wander out by themselves because of the danger of wild animals, however the scenery was beautiful, and the food was most enjoyable. Tabletop Range Park was escarpment country with waterfalls, and it was site of giant magnetic anthills up to four metres in height.

Arnhem Land and Kakadu were mainly Aboriginal areas, and the East Alligator River ran through them.

The next stop was at Broome to look at the very sandy beaches. Then they went on to Fitzroy Crossing and Halls Creek. The different shades of red in the countryside, with the intercepting green of the foliage, were amazing. When they rolled into Perth and were given a lovely room in a luxury motel, Margaret started to think of Gail and the children. It would be a great pleasure to see them all again. They spent some time in the gardens looking at the beautiful wild flowers that were native to Western Australia. The Kangaroo paws had such lovely colours and shapes.

They wandered in and out of the many shops and bought some gifts for the four grandchildren. The swan emblem was prominent on most of the little mementos. Margaret found a delightful cloth with two swans embroidered on it, which she bought for a thank-you gift for Denise for taking care of the animals. They were ready for their flight home and started wondering about the next school holidays, when they would spend more time with the children.

Andrew and Sandy took the three children to check Miska Valley once or twice, and everything appeared to be in order. They spoke to Peter, and Denise spent some time talking to Sandy. As usual Sandy looked beautiful in white shorts and a colourful blouse. Christie was growing up fast and becoming just as attractive as her mother.

"You will have to keep a lock and chain on your daughter, Sandy. The boys will be milling around," Denise noted.

"She does seem to have a very level head on her shoulders—thank goodness. But a little flirting doesn't do any harm. She wants to study law at university when the HSC is completed."

Peter and Denise were very impressed and wondered what road the twins would take. Denise spoke to Sandy later and asked her how the seminars were going. Sandy replied, "Still invigorating, and it's always good to meet new people and go to different places. Margaret and Richard will be home in a few days. I guess you will hear all about their trip."

"Yes, and we will be able to compare notes. I am looking forward to having morning tea with her," Denise replied.

When they left, Peter couldn't help saying what a beautiful lady Sandy was, but he felt that she couldn't be trusted. "Andrew must have rocks in his head if he can't see her hidden charms."

Chapter Sixteen

When the plane taxied to a standstill at Brisbane Airport, Richard and Margaret gathered their hand luggage and slowly manoeuvred to the waiting lounge, to be greeted by Andrew.

"How lovely to see you both looking so tanned and healthy, did you enjoy your trip?" their son asked.

"We had a wonderful time, Andrew. You will have to make time to take your family up there."

Andrew retrieved their luggage from the carousel and put it into his car. They were very excited to see their kittens and enjoy the peaceful home and gardens. They told Andrew that Richard had arranged to go with Peter to pick up their boat tomorrow so that he could take the children fishing during the school holidays. Richard had arranged the purchase with the dealer at the marine yard for the same boat and two motors that Peter had bought last year.

The shiny new boat was sitting on a trailer when the two men entered the yard, Richard's heart started to beat a little faster; he had wanted one for so long. They talked to the salesman about fishing gear and safety, along with the need to wear life jackets all the time when they were on the boat. Richard paid the cheque while Peter hooked the trailer up to the car. Richard couldn't wait to see the boy's faces and was not disappointed when Sandy dropped them off the next day.

"Gee Pa, what a surprise! Can we go fishing today?" Asked Scott & Jason in Unisom

Richard replied, "Yes. I will show you how to start the motor and also how to bait the hooks. Do you want to go fishing, Christie?"

"I think I would rather you take me for a little run on the lake. Then I will stay here with Nana."

The shore of the lake was low enough for the trailer to be driven into the water, and the boys winched the boat off. Then the trailer was put aside to wait for its return.

The boys had put on shorts, T-shirts, and hats. Then they put on the life jackets after Richard had instructed them about the motor. Christie wanted to know why David was not spending the school holidays with them. Margaret explained that he had gone on a school camp. Margaret suggested to Christie that they make some pies for when the fishermen came home.

When the men came to a spot on the lake where Richard thought the fish might be biting, he told Scott to stop the motor. "Now we will have to bait the hooks." He gave each boy a plastic held line so that they could release more line if the need arose. Jason felt a nibble on his line and gave a little tug, but the fish swam away. When the next fish swam near Scott, he jerked the line enough to make the fish grab at the bait, and he pulled the line in with a lovely perch on the end.

After sitting in the boat for about two hours, they had managed to catch three good-sized perch; they put the fish in the water bucket and headed home. Richard reversed the trailer with the Jeep until they could manoeuvre the boat onto it with the winch; Richard drove it out of the water and unhooked the trailer.

The boys were excited and ran over to Christie and Margaret with the bucket. "Look what we have caught, Nana. Will you cook them for dinner, please?"

While all the cleaning was going on, the boys started kicking a soccer ball around the yard. A small boy came over to join in the fun with Sally in tow. He introduced himself as Conner and said he was spending some time with his grandparents during the school holidays. Christie and Margaret prepared a bowl of salad and buttered some bread while Richard gutted and cleaned the fish ready for cooking

A short time later a very good-looking young man arrived on the scene and said that he was looking for his nephew, Conner. This was really just an excuse because he had seen a beautiful blonde girl whom he wanted to meet. The man introduced himself as Chad and said that he was Denise and Peter's grandson. He had sandy-coloured curls, brown eyes, and a tanned physique, which Christie found very interesting. He said, "I travel quite a lot with my job, so I don't get to see my grandparents very much."

"We are staying with our grandparents for part of the school holidays, and we are also helping out where we can," Christie said.

They talked for a few minutes, and then he called Conner and Sally and said that their dinner was ready. He said good-bye to everyone and told Christie that he hoped to see her again. When Chad spoke to Denise, he asked her if she would invite the Paterson family over for a BBQ tomorrow evening. "The young girl is beautiful," he commented.

Margaret and Richard had fired up their BBQ and were busy cooking the fish.

Scott remarked "The fish smells good and I am looking forward to some of that apple pie that Nana cooked too."

"What do you want to do tomorrow, children?" Richard asked.

"Can we go to see the whales from the cliff top?" Jason was very eager

"That is a good idea. We will drive through the bush again."

When the regular game of Scrabble was organized, the telephone rang. Denise invited the whole family to a BBQ dinner tomorrow. *Interesting*, thought Christie.

The children piled into the Jeep for the bumpy ride through the rough terrain in order to find the cliff road. It was quite a climb up the rocks to reach the top. They found their vantage points and waited in the hope of seeing the whales. They were not disappointed: a mother whale with her baby in tow splashed in and out of the water, having a great time. They sat on the cliff for a while to watch more activity from the huge monsters of the deep, they were migrating to feeding grounds.

Richard decided to drive on the well-paved roads to the local shopping centre to pick up some groceries for Margaret. Christie checked what was available in the little shops.

"The grass needs cutting, boys. Who will volunteer?"

Both boys wanted to drive the motor mower, so they tossed to see who would go first. Scott won, and Jason said that he would do a bit of weeding in the garden while he waited. Christie helped Nana to collect the washing from the line and fold it for putting away or ironing. The grandchildren had all taken to life at Miska Valley and loved to spend their holidays helping Pa and Nana. The boys were well into their studies; Jason was talking about studying economics, and Scott seemed to have his heart set on agriculture or engineering. Christie had made up her mind to study law and was putting every effort into study. The public school system had been kind to them: all of the subjects had been offered, and extra tutorage was always available when needed. David had been at an excellent private school in Brisbane, where he had majored in science. He wanted to study medicine when he started university next year.

The family dressed in casual gear to go to the Olson's' home next door/ Christie chose a pale blue bikini with a brightly coloured floral coverall, blue sandals, and a blue scarf in her hair. When Chad saw her, he gulped and stammered when he asked her if she would like something to drink.

Christie busied herself with putting a cloth on the table and setting the knives and forks for each person.

"Can I help you, Christie?" Chad offered.

"I can manage, thank you," she replied.

When the meal was finished and all the scraps were fed to Sally and Goldie, Chad asked Christie to go for a stroll around the property. He took her hand in his.

"Christie, you look so beautiful. I just had to get you alone so that I can get to know you. Denise tells me that you are still at school. What are your future plans?"

She said, "If my marks are good enough, I want to study law at university." She explained that she had a lot of study in front of her, but she also had a casual job at Target to help with pocket money. "I have been working most Thursday nights and Saturdays for the past three years. Dad said that I may have to give it up when I start university, but I hope not because I enjoy the companionship of the other staff."

Chad was amazed that such a beautiful girl had crossed his path, and even though her life was so full, he hoped that she could fit him in somewhere now and again. "Do you play any sport, like tennis, or do you watch soccer?" he asked.

"Yes, I do play a little tennis. I watch my brothers play soccer most weekends."

Christie felt a little tingle when Chad took her hand in his. She thought that his dark eyes were looking deep into her soul, and his cute curls needed to be messed up. He told her that his job took him away a lot to other countries as well as Australia, but he hoped to settle down eventually in Queensland. He told her about his brother Paul, his sister Kieran, and their children, including Conner and three little girls.

They decided to go to the movies the next day to see a very funny tale about a group of teenagers at a boarding school. Chad bought them some popcorn and a chocolate Magnum each to eat during the film, which she enjoyed immensely. Chad told Christie that he had to leave the next day to go to Sydney for his job, and he asked when she would be visiting again.

"Do you mind me asking you how old you are?" Christie was curious

"No, not at all, I am 22 and I have completed my university studies in Marketing." Christie thought that her mother would be happy with these facts.

"My grandparents are making up for lost time when they had to work so hard in their furniture business. Now they are travelling quite a bit."

"You will have to give me your mobile number. I will give you mine so that we can keep in touch." Chad wrote his number on a slip of paper and gave it to her; she returned the favour.

They went for a drive to the beach and found a small café, where they decided to have raisin toast and coffee. Chad was gazing across the table at her and couldn't resist telling her once more how beautiful she was. She told him that she thought that he was gorgeous as well, and she mentioned how nice it was that they had found each other to spend a little time together, even if it was only for a short time.

When they arrived back at Miska Valley, Margaret was a little concerned, however Chad assured her that he had taken good care of her granddaughter and was returning her safely. He gave Margaret a kiss on her cheek, and he gave Christie a big hug and a kiss. He said, "Till we meet again."

"Oh, dear Young love," exclaimed Margaret.

"Don't worry, Nana. I think he is gorgeous, but I know that I have a lot on my plate for now."

Christie told her mother about meeting Chad at Denise's place. Sandy thought that she would have to check him out. *Can't have my daughter wasting her time on a nobody. I will have to teach her a few moves for the future, and I'll make sure that she is on the pill.* Sandy made a note in her diary so that she remembered to keep a good check on her daughter; she couldn't have Christie outshining her. Her thoughts then turned to Glenn and when she would be seeing him again. She looked at her diary for the next seminar. *February, Won't be long now,* She smiled and floated away in a dream of what might happen.

Chapter Seventeen

~◦◦❦◦◦~

Sandy was reminded by her boss that she was required to attend the next seminar at Redcliff Motel in February. They had been working on a new cream to help stop aging wrinkles, and they wanted to get it on the market before rival companies had a chance to beat them. After speaking to Andrew, she asked Margaret if she could stay at her place for one night because Andrew said that he could manage the rest of the time with the help of the kids. Sandy felt that Christie was old enough to take responsibility for a lot of the household, but she was always mindful of Gail's remarks about children's needs. Christie was completing her last year at high school, and Andrew was very mindful of her workload; he hadn't met Chad yet but had heard a lot about him from his daughter.

"Just remember that your studies have to come first," Andrew told his daughter.

"Yes, Dad, Chad is away a lot with his job, but he is good company. I will introduce you next time he comes over to see me."

Sandy kissed the family and bid them farewell on Wednesday. She drove off with an air of excitement floating dangerously around her. She had packed a few extra towels and another special bikini in the hope that Glenn would be there. She wasn't disappointed. He drove in behind her, and she jumped out of her car and suggested to him that they skip the seminar and drive to a secluded spot at the beach, where they could book into a small suite for two nights. Glenn was very interested but also very hesitant. They drove away in Sandy's car, leaving Glenn's car parked in the hotel parking area.

"Sandy, I can't risk blowing my cover. You seem to have great trust in your family."

"Never mind Glenn, I will book the suite, and we will come here after dinner."

Sandy had a look at the suite: one bedroom, a large bathroom with a sizeable bathtub and shower, and a lovely queen-sized bed with plenty of soft cushions. She didn't particularly want to attend the lectures, so she texted Glenn with the address and said that she expected him between 9:00 and 10:00 p.m. Glenn spent a miserable day half listening to the speaker and wondering what Sandy would get up to.

When he found the address, he parked his car and then knocked softly on the door. He heard a voice telling him to come in; the door was not locked. He followed the discarded clothes that were strewn over the floor, and he wandered into the large bathroom to find a beautiful "mermaid" floating amid soap bubbles that threatened to bounce over the edge of the top of the bath. Her blonde hair and blue eyes could just be seen peeping over the froth.

"Hello, sexy," she purred. "Come and join me."

Glenn discarded his clothes and slowly slithered into the warm water, splashing some bubbles on the floor. "This is heaven, Sandy, so beautiful and warm."

They kissed each other and proceeded to wash each other in a sensuous manner until their lust took over. They climbed out to have a shower and wash away the bubbles. They fell into a sound sleep when they finally pulled the bed covers over their naked bodies.

"Sandy, can we do that all again tomorrow night?"

"Yes, my love. Once is not enough."

When Glenn crept out to return for his breakfast in the motel, Sandy looked around the suite, remembered what had occurred, and smiled to herself. *Yes, Glenn,* she thought. *I will keep last night in my dreams for some time.* She dressed, tidied up the suite, and then went in search of a light breakfast at a little café. The small gathering of shops was beckoning, and she spent an hour or two trying on some gorgeous dresses and tops that were quite different to clothes in the big shops. Her next purchase was a book on fiction, a love story that made her both sad and happy. *This could be my story,* she thought. *I wonder how many women have two l*

She decided to give Margaret a ring to see how she was coping, and of course the call would register on her bill from Redcliff. *Have to keep tracks covered,* she thought. Her evening meal was lonely, but thinking of what would happen after helped to make it enjoyable.

Glenn arrived a little earlier, telling her that he had told the seminar people that he was going home a little earlier because one of the children was not well.

"Do you think that was a good idea, Glenn?" Sandy asked him.

"It will be okay. If Carol needs to ring me, she will ring on the mobile. I just have to spend more time with my mermaid!"

Sandy went to the bathroom to fill the bath with bubbles again. They argued a bit about who would be on top and splashed the bubbles about, and it was such fun. Sandy told Glenn about Christie meeting a very handsome older boy at Miska Valley. He was twenty-two and travelled a lot with his job, but Christie seemed to be more than interested.

Their lovemaking was so erotic and exhaustive that they slept until the sun woke them when it came creeping around the curtains. They dressed, packed their backpacks, and put them in the cars. They decided to find a little cafe out of town, and then they would head home. Glenn went into a jewellery shop and came out with a little box. He gave it to Sandy, and she opened it to find a gold mermaid on a charm so that she could wear it on her Pandora bracelet.

"I have tried not to fall in love with you, Sandy. We both know that our love can never be anything more than what we have now."

"Yes, Glenn. Thank you. I will wear it always."

Sandy knew that she would have to end their affair because Glenn was becoming too serious, and she could not afford to jeopardise her marriage to Andrew. Andrew may not be the best lover in the world, but he was trusting and reliable and she did love him. They said good-bye, got into their own cars, and drove home. Her heart was heavy, but she knew that her decision to end their affair was the right thing to do for everybody concerned. She would think about the best way to make the break. Maybe she'd text him, or she may talk to him on his mobile. She spent a lot of time making the right decision. *I hope he doesn't feel that it is necessary to confess to Carol. That would ruin everything.*

Sandy decided that she would have to find another job, perhaps in fashion or maybe a shoe line. The possibilities were endless—so long as they had seminars to attend.

Margaret had already left when Sandy arrived home. The children were always pleased to see her and wanted to know what was on the menu for dinner. She decided to ring Andrew and arrange for them to go to their favourite seafood restaurant. The meal was enjoyable, and then they spent some time watching a short movie before heading home for the boys to have a sound sleep before soccer in the morning.

Gail had had a gruelling two weeks with a family who had been neglecting one of their children. The little boy of six had become so thin that a teacher made a complaint to Docs. Gail had visited the home and found it hard to believe that they could lavish so much love on the other two children but not Paul. She asked Connie if she could tell her what the problem was, but she just burst into tears. The problem seemed to accelerate over time. Everything that Paul tried to do ended up the wrong way, and then the other two laughed at him—little things like holding a pencil and tying his own shoelaces. The other two children were older and younger, one a girl and the other a boy. Michael was at a loss to explain it; he said that he loved all three children equally and tried to encourage Paul to eat more of his food and join in with the games that his sister and brother had fun playing. Gail felt that a nutritionist was needed and told Connie to take him to a local doctor. She spent a lot of time with the family and the doctor had Paul tested for autism, which proved to be correct. He had to be enrolled into a special school that would help him over the years. It was always a worry when a child started to withdraw from brothers and sisters, and the parents couldn't seem to help.

Gail spent a little more time with her parents at Miska Valley. She went fishing with her father to catch some more freshwater perch, which Richard cooked on the BBQ. Margaret made a lovely fresh salad to eat with them. Gail wandered around the garden looking at the flowers, and Denise spotted her and started to talk. Denise asked where Sandy had gone on her last seminar, and Gail told her that she did not know, but Gail didn't see much of Sandy, and Andrew seemed very happy. Brett had to stay to manage the motel while Gail was away. David did take his turn on a regular basis, which gave them more time to spend together these days. The tourists were becoming more regular, and even though the motel was not close to the beach, it was a good place to have a break on the highway after a long trip from Sydney or Melbourne.

David was looking at five years at university to get a medical degree, and so the hours spent at the motel gave him his pocket money. He helped with the bookwork for the monthly returns and any other manual work that his father had for him. Brett thought he may be able to find some work for the twins now that Richard had taught them about machinery; it was far better than playing games on iPads and other gadgets. Brett loved to do the gardening around the motel, and he took great pride in the gardens. The visitors always commented about the beautiful natives and often asked him how he managed to keep them looking so healthy.

David had met a very pretty girl at university. Her name was Jessica, and she hoped to become a doctor also. They studied together sometimes, and she had a casual job at a big department store in Brisbane. Because of all the commitments they had, their private lives were restricted to casual dating. They talked about long-term possibilities, such as specializing in some field and also using their skills overseas, but one thing stayed the same: they would end up as a married couple. Brett and Gail liked the idea; they felt that Jessica was a lovely girl, and when the time was right after all their studies, they would make a go of it.

Brett thought of Christie and how they were all growing up so fast. *I guess we will be grandparents before long. That could be interesting.* Margaret and Richard would love it.

Chapter Eighteen

C hristie had been researching for an assignment when a message appeared on her mobile. "In BrisbaneCan we meet? CO."

She thought about it for a few minutes and decided to reply. "Tomorrow p.m." It would be good to see Chad again, as long as he didn't want to make it too often.

She had made arrangements to meet a girlfriend at the library in George Street in the afternoon; she would meet Chad there at the same time. The library was the best place to find answers to the many questions that arose in her courses about law, and she found it stimulating. Fiona was waiting for her when she walked in to the foyer. They made enquiries with the mature lady at the desk as to where the best places were to research their subjects. After the tasks were completed, Christie told Fiona about meeting Chad when they were ready to leave. Fiona was a little surprised to hear that she had a boyfriend, but Christie explained that she had met him at Miska Valley, when she was staying with her grandparents.

"He is a little older than me. He took me to see a movie and to a cafe."

"Very interesting Christie what did your grandmother think of him?"

"She likes him but made sure that he realised that I am younger and have a lot of study in front of me over the next few years." She looked up. "Oh, here he is now. Chad, I would like you to meet my good friend Fiona."

Fiona shook his hand and said how pleased she was to meet him. She looked at Christie and winked to let her know that she approved. The three of them walked to a small café, where Christie and Chad shared a cup of coffee and learnt a little more about each other. Chad asked Christie when she was going to visit her grandparents again, and he was disappointed to learn that she wouldn't be there until later in the year, after she had finished her final exams. The girls said that they had some shopping to do and asked Chad when he was going away again. He replied he was leaving tomorrow and he wouldn't be back until next month.

"I will give you a ring when I get home, Christie. Take care." Chad said good-bye to Fiona and then kissed Christie on the cheek before leaving.

Fiona couldn't help herself and said to Christie, "He is gorgeous, Christie! Don't let him run away."

"I have a lot on my plate, Fiona. We will have to see if he is willing to wait." The girls finished all of their shopping and caught a bus home to tackle some of their assignments.

Christie spoke to her father about dating Chad. He thought about his quick marriage, and even though it had worked out in the long run, he didn't want his daughter to have a situation like that. She had years of study in front of her. He advised her to play it cool with casual dates. He also believed that Chad still had more studies to complete his management degree.

"Why don't you contact your cousin and ask him if he will consider double dating now and again?"

"That is a good idea, Dad. I will give David a call."

When she rang David, he agreed as long as Jessica was okay with the idea. When Chad contacted her at the end of the month, she explained the situation. He thought it a little strange and said that he wanted to spend time alone with her. She said that there was safety in numbers, and that was the way she wanted to move forward. The first arrangement was to a university get-together, which would give Christie a good idea of how students socialized.

When David introduced Jessica, Christie was very impressed with her long, golden blonde hair and green eyes. She was not very tall, was very slim, and obviously adored David. Chad was a little put out as to the place of the date, but he realised that it was Christie's way of protecting herself, and he decided to go along with it.

The twins went to stay with Nana and Pa during the next school holidays, and Richard was very pleased with the way that they handled the chores. He spent a lot of time fishing with them and off-road driving, which they enjoyed immensely. He told them, "I will teach you how to drive a car next time you visit."

Life was good for Richard and Margaret. They had visited the young couple at Banora Point and found that the furniture business was still flourishing. Goldie was living at the valley full time, and the three cats were thoroughly spoilt. That was the way Margaret wanted it.

The four friends continued to date. They had lovely picnics in the beautiful Roma Street parkland and the Brisbane botanic gardens on a regular basis. The university hosted a ball, and the girls dressed in their finery and danced the night away. Chad was very impressed with Jessica. Christie knew that David was very confident in their relationship; they had talked about their future plans, and they both needed part-time jobs to help make the future more secure.

Christie and Fiona joined in with most of the social events that were organized at the school. They spent most Saturdays at the tennis courts. Fiona was a better player than Christie, which meant that her time was taken up more as the finals approached.

Christie decided to visit her grandparents just before Christmas to help Nana do some baking for the big dinner at the valley. All the family would be in attendance, and Jessica had been invited too. Chad wandered over during the afternoon to say hello and to ask her if she would like to go to a restaurant and a movie during the holidays. She gave him a big hug and kiss, thanking him for the invitation. Then they spent the afternoon talking about their plans for the following year.

Christmas Day dawned with a brilliant sunrise that spread across the eastern sky. Andrew, Sandy, and the boys arrived early with their brand-new roller skates to try on the paths. Gail and Brett managed to find a willing helper to man the office at the motel for a couple of hours so that they could spend part of the day with the family. David and Jessica arrived hand in hand, with Jessica displaying her beautiful heart-shaped locket that David had given her as a present. Christie hoped that Chad would come to visit later in the day. They enjoyed a scrumptious meal of roasted turkey and vegetables, with plum pudding for dessert. When all the dishes were loaded into the dishwasher, the present giving was started. Andrew gave Sandy a lovely pair of diamond earrings, and Brett gave Gail a sapphire and diamond bracelet. Everyone admired the gifts, and the entire family gave a large water feature to Margaret and Richard.

Sandy had spoken to Glenn to tell him that their liaison was finished, and he should not contact her in the future. However, she couldn't help fiddling with the little gold mermaid on her Pandora bracelet.

Chad wandered through the trees late in the afternoon. He shook hands with the men and put his arm around Christie to give her a kiss. They wandered away with their hands tightly clasped to sit on a bench near the pool. He gave Christie a small package wrapped in pink paper and tied with a blue ribbon. She opened it to find a lovely friendship ring, which he put on her ring finger on her right hand. The little emerald blinked in the sunshine, and he told her that he felt he was falling in love with her. He promised to stand by her in all her studies in the near future. Christie was thrilled, and she threw her arms around his neck and gave him a big kiss. She had chosen a pair of gold cufflinks for him to wear on important meetings.

The day finished with everyone having a swim and then returning home to wait for the New Year celebrations.

The Brisbane City Council always put on a brilliant fireworks display on the bank of the river in front of the building, which was enjoyed by all and was shown on television. All of the teenagers had a lovely time watching the display and wandering around the city until midnight, when a loud cheer went up to welcome the New Year. Jason and Scott were escorted home, and then the four friends went along to a movie that had been advertised.

Christie received her exams results and also her university entrance grades. She was offered a placing in the university that was midway between the Gold Coast and Miska Valley. She was thrilled and rang Andrew to tell him the great news. She also asked him if he could spare the money to buy her a car to travel to and from school for the next five years. Andrew and Sandy were more than happy to help her.

Chapter Nineteen

———❦———

Margaret had been to the craft group with Denise during the morning, and they had been working on a project for the upcoming bazaar at the church. The design for the quilt was very complicated with a lot of very small pieces forming squares and triangles. It was coming together, and they hoped that they could finish next week. Denise said good-bye to Margaret and drove to her home for lunch.

Margaret walked into her home and called out to Richard. "I am home! Where are you?" He did not answer, so she thought that he must be out in the garden. She spent some time looking around. To her horror she found him slumped over the riding lawnmower in the shed. She screamed and eased him on to the floor. He opened his eyes and then tried to get up.

"Oh, my darling, whatever is the matter? I must ring for an ambulance," she said. "Please stay still. I have my mobile here, and I have dialled triple zero."

The ambulance seemed to take forever to arrive, by which time Margaret was distraught. She didn't want to leave him, so she rang Denise and Peter to come over to help. Peter managed to start CPR, and Margaret rang Andrew to tell him that they would be at the hospital. The medics were very kind, and when they thought that they had stabilised Richard, they loaded him into the ambulance and transported him to the hospital. Margaret went with him and left Peter to lock up.

Richard's face was ashen, and the medics kept working on him. Margaret tried her best not to cry; she had to keep strong for her love of over sixty years. The sirens were blazing and the lights were flashing when they pulled into the emergency parking area. Thankfully Andrew was waiting, and Margaret fell into his arms as the tears came.

"What happened to him, Mum? Has he had a heart attack?'

"I don't know. I found him in the shed and rang the ambulance."

Andrew told her that he had rung Gail while he was waiting. The doctors and nurses rushed Richard into emergency, so Andrew and Margaret sat in the small waiting room for information. Gail and Brett arrived, and Gail hugged her mother. Andrew and Brett walked a short distance away to talk; Andrew said that Sandy was shopping, but he had left a message on her mobile. Sandy did arrive shortly afterwards and rushed into Andrew's arms, wanting to know how Richard was.

The doctor came out, but he didn't look happy. "Your father has had a major heart attack. We are doing everything possible, but it will be a hard fight for him." Margaret fell into a chair and started to cry. Gail and Sandy did their best to comfort her.

"Can we see him?" Andrew asked.

"You may go in, but he is not conscious."

Margaret sat in a chair beside his bed and held his hand. She spoke to him very quietly to let him know that she was there, and silent tears ran down her cheeks. When Andrew and Gail felt that they could not help any more, they spoke to the sister in charge and asked her to ring if there was any change in his condition.

Richard opened his eyes some time later, saw Margaret there, and squeezed her hand.

"Oh, Richard, I am so glad. You did give such a fright. Do you want anything, dear?"

Unfortunately he was not capable of answering and drifted back into unconsciousness. She sat there until late in the night, when Andrew and Gail returned.

Andrew said, "Mum, you need to have something to eat. Gail will take you for a meal, and I will stay here with Dad."

Margaret let Gail lead her away, but she said that she would be back as soon as possible. She told Gail that he had had a check-up only last week, and everything was okay. She told Gail that she would not leave the hospital without Richard. This statement upset Gail, but she understood how she felt after sixty years together. Sandy had told the children, and Gail had told David. They all wanted to come and visit and were told that they could visit tomorrow if all was going well.

The early hours of the new day were not kind. Richard slipped away, the monitor started beeping, and doctors and nurses rushed from everywhere. They started using the defibrillator but without success. Richard had passed away. Gail and Andrew held Margaret until she had stopped sobbing, and then they led her to an office, where arrangements were made with the authorities to take charge of the body.

Christie was terribly upset and insisted on spending the day with Margaret to help in any way that she could.

The three boys stayed with Sandy for most of the day. "What will happen to Nana?" they asked. This was their main concern.

They decided that Margaret would stay with Sandy tonight and till after the funeral. Then other arrangements would have to be made. Sandy was starting to run ideas through her head, mainly to do with money.

The White Ladies Funeral Home was contacted to make all the arrangements for a service to be held at the crematorium in two days' time. Andrew and Gail read eulogies on their father's life, and Christie read a special one on behalf of the three boys and herself, saying how much Richard had helped them to grow up into adults.

Their close friends and business associates paid their respects and stayed for a wake after the service.

Gail, Brett, Andrew, and Sandy sat down to talk about the best solution for all concerned. Margaret had to be looked after, and nobody wanted to sell Miska Valley. It was decided that Andrew and Sandy and the twins could move to the valley, and the boys would have to commute to school by bus each day. Gail and Brett would have to stay where they were, close to Gail's work. Andrew and Sandy would rent their home and use the money to pay the mortgage on the house. There was no immediate rush, so Christie said that she would move to Miska Valley to help Nana. The rest of the family could move in at the end of the month. Christie set herself up in the third bedroom.

When they all moved to Miska Valley, Sandy and Andrew moved into the second bedroom, and the boys moved into the guest house. Sandy thought the arrangements were stupid. Margaret didn't need the biggest bedroom anymore. However, life progressed with Margaret joining Denise to go to craft and other outings. Sandy was getting more and more agitated with the sleeping arrangements, trying not to show her displeasure. *I will wait for my opportunity,* she thought.

The three women took it in turns to cook and clean. The boys and Andrew did the outside chores. Andrew told the boys that they had to wait until he was home before they rode on the mower. Everything appeared to be working out well, and Margaret was enjoying herself once more even though she still missed Richard a lot.

Christie had started to commute to the university. She was so excited, and maybe she would see Chad now and again.

Christie's prayers were answered when she saw Chad striding across the grass towards the guest house.

"Hello, Christie. Nana told me that you were living here now. I was so sorry to hear about Richard. He was such a nice guy. Can you fit a movie date into your busy schedule?"

"Yes, Chad, that would be lovely. Thank you."

Sandy saw the two of them talking and wondered who the spunky guy was. She thought of an excuse to go to the guest house so that she could be introduced.

"Gee," Chad said. "I can see where your looks come from."

Sandy talked to Chad for some time and decided that Christie knew how to pick them.

University proved to be a real eye opener for Christie with all the lectures she had to attend, and with many assignments to be completed for each teacher. She enjoyed her work and spent many hours shut inside her room to study. Chad had only been home for a few days, but they made time to swim, sit, and talk a lot, holding hands whenever they had the chance. Sandy wanted to know if he had kissed her yet or had made advances. Christie told her mother to mind her own business.

Gail made visits to see how her mother was coping. The arrangement was okay, and the boys managed to keep the pool clean and fresh. The Jeep didn't go anywhere and was waiting for the twins to learn to drive, but Andrew felt that it was too powerful for them and decided to sell it.

The boat remained on the trailer, but Andrew felt that he would take it out when he was on holidays soon; some fresh fish would be nice. Goldie looked for Richard for some time but seemed content with the boys' company.

The three cats were getting quite big, but they were still very playful. Pebbles still slept with Christie, and Shadow and Shannon crept in there whenever no one was looking.

Chad asked Christie to go to Sydney for a weekend. She asked Sandy what she thought, and her mother's reply was to take her chances when she could but not to forget the condoms. Sandy felt that now her daughter had had her eighteenth birthday, she should learn what life was all about. She packed a little overnight bag and put it into Chad's car. The car was a small Volkswagen with black upholstery. Christie felt at home sitting there; she liked driving her own car but Chad's car was much more luxurious. *After Dad has sold the Jeep, the twins will pester him for cars of their own they can practise on Mum's Astra.*

Chad and Christie headed down the Pacific Highway and then onto the M1, (Motorway One) which took them into North Sydney. Chad had booked a room in a medium-range motel. They went to a stylish restaurant for a gourmet dinner, drinking some wine with the meal. Chad took Christie for a walk over the harbour Bridge and to see the sights at Circular Quay. She was fascinated by all the buskers: some were singing with beautiful voices, and some were acrobats and vying for attention too. The night was so much fun, and Chad told her that he would take her to Bondi Beach in the morning.

When they got back to the motel, they decided to have a swim in the pool, followed by a shower and a warm cuddle on the big sofa. Chad slid his arm around her shoulder and started to rub her breasts. She decided that it felt good and could see no reason to tell him to stop. When he pulled her onto her back, she asked him if he had protection and then let her desire take over.

After the trip to Bondi Beach and a fish and chips lunch, the long drive home was in front of them. He told her, "Christie, you are the most beautiful girl. I hope that we can have many more weekends over the years while you are doing your course." They stopped again to have a light lunch of hamburger and salad, and they drove on the coast roads to see the sights.

When they drove into Miska Valley, Sandy was dying to ask her if she was still a virgin. Her curiosity would have to wait for another day or two. Life was never easy.

Chapter Twenty

Sandy took her opportunity when Andrew had to go to Perth for a few days on business. She told Margaret that they were too crowded with the sleeping arrangements the way they were, and she wanted Margaret to move into the guest house and take all her possessions with her. Sandy and Andrew would move into the main bedroom with the en suite. Christie would move into the big queen-size room, and the boys could share the third bedroom. That way Sandy could keep a better eye on what the boys were doing.

"But, Sandy, that is not what Richard wanted for me," Margaret protested.

"Too bad Richard isn't here anymore. Please tell Andrew and Gail that the new arrangement is far more sensible."

Margaret was distraught, but Sandy said that if she didn't like it, Sandy would leave, and Margaret would not see the children again. Margaret remembered a remark that Denise had said to her not long after she had been talking to Sandy: it was about Sandy's jealousy of Gail and the way she ran after lazy parents' kids and never her own niece or nephews. *Perhaps I will just have to make the best of it. I do love the children so much and would be devastated if I couldn't see them.*

Sandy packed all of Margaret's little knick-knacks into boxes and put them into the guest house.

When Christie arrived home from school, she wanted to know why Nana had moved all her belongings into the guest house. Sandy explained that it made Margaret more independent; she could come and go without having to disturb anyone, and her car was parked right outside her door. Christie didn't like the arrangement but felt that her mother must know best. The boys accepted their mother's reasons. Sandy thought that Andrew had stopped her from spending time with her own interests and had more or less tied her to Miska Valley. She would now live the way she chose. *If Gail wants to visit, there is nowhere for her to stay overnight. Margaret is still capable of looking after herself. I will ask her to eat with the family once or twice a week, and she can still manage her own laundry.*

Sandy was thinking about her mother, Pam, and what she would have done if she had been confronted with these circumstances. *Andrew is not a problem—he just goes along with the flow so long as his personal needs are taken care of. The boys are more than happy with life in general; they do miss Richard, but it won't be long until they can drive the Jeep and the boat.* Christie was a concern because she had really taken to her grandparents, however Sandy would handle the situation if it arose.

Christie spoke to her grandmother about the arrangements, and Margaret told her not to worry because she could manage all right. Christie could see that Margaret was upset but was trying not to show it. Christie decided to talk to Denise in confidence as soon as she could.

When Andrew arrived back from Perth, he was startled to see the changes that had been made, and he decided to talk to his mother. "When did the living arrangements change, Mum?"

"Sandy and I discussed the crowded living quarters, and we decided that I would be comfortable in the guest house."

"Are you sure that you don't mind?"

"I will be okay, Andrew. I just want to be near you all."

Andrew thought about the situation and put his mind at rest knowing that Sandy would do the right thing by all concerned. *She always does.*

Christie had a talk with Denise to find out what if anything Margaret had told her about the changes. Denise remarked that her grandmother didn't want to rock the boat, but she was upset. Christie decided to let the situation remain as was, but she would keep her eyes and ears open.

When Margaret told Christie that Sandy wanted Margaret to sign her legal papers over to Sandy and not Andrew, Christie became alarmed and decided to find someone to talk to without her mother knowing about it. Gail was always busy with the disadvantaged children. Christie consulted the help pages in the telephone book to make an appointment with a person who could advise her on what she could do to help her grandmother. Margaret, with Christie's advice, arranged a consultation with a solicitor in Brisbane. The two of them spent some time talking to a very understanding man regarding what they could do about the situation. He suggested that Andrew should come to see him with Margaret and Sandy.

Christie remembered a telephone call from a lady by the name of Amelia from Coffs Harbour. Amelia had wanted to contact her mother about a cosmetic conference, and Sandy had been annoyed about Amelia ringing her home phone number. Christie remembered leaving the note, with Amelia's number on it, in the pocket of her slacks. *I wonder if I can find it?.* Sure enough, it was still there. *I will have to tell Dad to say something to Mum, because I think Mum is treating Nana shamefully.*

Christie decided to ring Amelia to find out what she wanted her mother for. Amelia said that some of her friends were asking about Sandy because she hadn't been to the last seminar. Christie asked Amelia the date of the last seminar, which was the date her mother had gone on her last trip. *Something is wrong here,* she thought, but she did not want to cause problems between her parents. *I will ask Mum quietly, to get an answer.*

"Why did you not go to the seminar in February, Mum? You drove away somewhere?" she said to Sandy.

"Yes, I did go to the seminar. Why do you ask such a silly question?"

"Mum, I have spoken to Amelia. For some reason you are not telling the truth."

Sandy lost her temper and shouted at Christie. She told her to mind her own business, and said if Christie told any lies to Andrew, she would be very sorry.

Christie had expected this outburst and replied, "I don't want to know what you were doing in February, and I don't intend to say anything to Dad—if you put Nana back into her own room and treat her as you should."

Sandy told Christie that she had no right to speak to her that way, but she agreed to make the necessary changes as soon as possible.

When Sandy had restored Margaret to her own room she sat quietly for awhile to think about what she had done. *Maybe it is all for the best, Andrew could never know about Glenn and she felt sure that Pam would have handled the situation better.*

Christie told Sandy that their relationship may remain strained for awhile, however she would do her best to forget the incident and get on with her studies.